THE KID WHO ★ BECAME ★ PRESIDENT

If you like

THE KID WHO BECAME PRESIDENT

you'll *love* Dan Gutman's
other hilarious books:

THE KID WHO RAN FOR PRESIDENT

THEY CAME FROM CENTERFIELD

TALES FROM THE SANDLOT #1:
THE SHORTSTOP WHO KNEW TOO MUCH

TALES FROM THE SANDLOT #2:
THE GREEN MONSTER IN LEFT FIELD

TALES FROM THE SANDLOT #3:
THE CATCHER WHO SHOCKED
THE WORLD

TALES FROM THE SANDLOT #4:
THE PITCHER WHO WENT OUT OF
HIS MIND

THE KID WHO

★ BECAME ★

PRESIDENT

Sequel to THE KID WHO RAN FOR PRESIDENT

DAN GUTMAN

AN
APPLE
PAPERBACK

NEW YORK TORONTO LONDON AUCKLAND SYDNEY
MEXICO CITY NEW DELHI HONG KONG BUENOS AIRES

No part of this publication may be reproduced, stored in a retrieval system, or transmitted in any form or by any means, electronic, mechanical, photocopying, recording, or otherwise, without written permission of the publisher. For information regarding permission, write to Scholastic Inc., Attention: Permissions Department, 557 Broadway, New York, NY 10012.

ISBN-13: 978-0-590-02376-4
ISBN-10: 0-590-02376-4

23 22 21 20 19 18 17 16 15   8 9 10 11 12/0

Printed in the U.S.A.   40
First Scholastic printing, November 1999

★

Dedicated to all the kids who inspired me at schools I visited in 1998 . . .

In New Jersey: Whitman School in Turnersville, Friends School in Haddonfield, Appleby School in Spottswood, #1 School in West New York, Wood School in Millville, Memorial School in Pitman, Adams School in Cape May, Moorestown School in Moorestown, Hillside School in Mt. Laurel, Carson School in Pennsauken, Bean and Glenn Schools in Pine Hill, Harmony Township School in Phillipsburg, Hillsborough School in Belle Mead, Miller School in Kinnelon, Memorial School in Cinnaminson, DeWolf School in Old Tappan, Highland School in Midland Park, Logan Township School in Swedesboro, Birches School in Turnersville, Lower Alloways Creek School in Salem, Packanack School in Wayne, Yellin School in Stratford, Rice School in Marlton, Port Republic School in Port Republic, Sewell School in Sewell, Sunnybrae School in Yardville, Penns Grove School in Penns Grove, Antheil School in Trenton, Broad Street School in Gibbstown, Central School in East Hanover, Hillside School in Bridgewater, Somerdale Park School in Somerdale, Desmares School in Flemington.

In Pennsylvania: Crooked Billet and Pennypack Schools in Hatboro, Kulp School in Hatfield, Lincoln Park School in West Lawn, Rush School in Bensalem, Chadds Ford School in Chadds Ford, Coebourn School in Brookhaven, Arcola School in Norristown, West Broad Street and Oak Ridge Schools in Souderton, Garnet Valley School in Glen Mills.

In New York State: Bedford Village School in Bedford, P.S. 139 in Rego Park, Mamaroneck School in Mamaroneck, Brookside School in Ossining, Hillcrest School in Peekskill, Furnace Woods School in Cortlandt Manor.

Also, West Blocton and Woodstock Schools in West Blocton, Alabama, and Northwest School in Ankeny, Iowa.

★ **Contents** ★

THE KID WHO

★ **BECAME** ★

PRESIDENT

★ Prologue ★
The Big Flip-flop

At exactly noon on January 20, I stood before the world, raised my right hand, and recited the following words:

> *"I, Judson Moon, do solemnly swear that I will faithfully execute the Office of President of the United States, and will, to the best of my ability, preserve, protect, and defend the Constitution of the United States."*

They say that in America *any* kid — rich or poor, black or white — can become President. Well, I was the kid who *did*.

The moment I finished taking the oath of office that day, I was no longer a plain old thirteen-year-old from Madison, Wisconsin. I was the leader of the free world. I was the most powerful person on the planet.

How did it happen? If you've read a book called *The Kid Who Ran for President*, you know the incredible, improbable events that led up to me winning the last election. If you didn't, that's okay.

To make a long story short, I was hanging around with my friend Lane Brainard after school one day when he jokingly suggested that a kid would make a good President of the United States. A kid like me. As a goof, I went along with the idea.

Things kind of snowballed after that. Lane is a true genius, and he figured out how to raise millions of dollars to finance my campaign. He told me what to do, how to act, and what to say. He designed the bumper stickers and T-shirts. He directed the TV commercials. He even figured out how to get a constitutional amendment passed that would allow any American, regardless of age, to run for President.

We got some breaks. The Democratic candidate that year happened to be an idiot. The Republican was a jerk. People seemed to like me for my goofy sense of humor and devil-may-care attitude. That, plus the fact that I have very good hair. The next thing I knew, I was ahead in the polls.

By the time I fully realized that my candidacy wasn't all a big practical joke, it was too late. The Judson Moon for President campaign was like a runaway train. On election night, the American people chose me to be the youngest President in American history. I can hardly believe it really happened.

Then, the night I won the election, I resigned. That's right, I quit. I got on TV and basically yelled at America for being so *stupid* as to elect a kid President of the United States. Everybody was totally blown away that someone would turn down the chance to be President. My mother passed out on national television.

Well, my fellow Americans, I'm here to say that I had a change of heart. Politicians do that all the time, you know. It's called a flip-flop. One day you believe one thing, and the next day you take the opposite point of view. It's human nature. People change.

Anyway, I decided to accept the presidency after all. This book is the story of my presidency.

Can a kid — an innocent seventh-grader like me — make a good President? Or did the job totally overwhelm me and make me fall on my face, humiliating me and the office of the President? If you'd like, you can turn to page 215 and see what happened.

That is, if you're a pea brain who has to have instant gratification.

If I were you, I'd read the book. You might actually enjoy it.

But it's up to you. This is still a free country.

— Judson Moon

1.
★ **A Chance** ★

The moment I told America I was refusing the presidency, pandemonium broke loose at the Moon for President headquarters in the grand ballroom of the Edgewater Hotel in Madison, Wisconsin. That's the town I live in. In the two centuries since George Washington was elected our first President, no candidate had *ever* used his acceptance speech to say he didn't want the job after all.

Cameras flashed like fireworks. Reporters went running to the telephones to call their newspapers and change the headlines from **MOON WINS!** to **MOON WINS...AND QUITS!** Television guys were elbowing each other out of the way trying to get to me for interviews.

My friend and campaign manager, Lane Brainard, just stared at me with his mouth open.

The girl I had chosen to be my "first babe"— Chelsea Daniels — started screaming as if she'd seen a monster.

My mom was in shock. She had to be taken to the hospital.

Some people thought I was joking. Others were crying. People were running around as if somebody had pulled the fire alarm. Everybody was acting like the world was coming to an end.

I just laughed. I stood at the podium, watching everything swirl around me, and laughed. It was such a relief that the election was over, I didn't care what happened. I never really wanted to be President in the first place.

That night, when all the excitement had died down and I went home, there was a soft knock at the front door. I opened it and Mrs. June Syers wheeled herself in.

Mrs. Syers had been my baby-sitter when I was a little boy. She was old now and so crippled by Parkinson's disease that she needed a wheelchair to get around. Her mind was sharp, though, maybe the sharpest of any grown-up I knew. When Lane had asked me to select a grown-up to run as my Vice-President, I picked Mrs. Syers right away.

"Moon, you do have a way of surprising folks," she chuckled.

"I'm sorry," I replied. "I kind of messed things up for you, didn't I?"

If I had accepted the presidency, Mrs. Syers would have been the first African-American and the first female Vice-President in American history. I felt bad about depriving her of that honor.

"Forget it, Moon."

"I know what you're going to say," I told her as I wheeled her into the living room. "You're going to say I'm crazy. You're going to say I was always crazy. And I always *will* be crazy. Right?"

"No," Mrs. Syers replied. "That ain't what I was gonna say."

"Then, what?"

"Child, when I was born, women weren't even allowed to vote yet. At your age, I couldn't eat in a restaurant where white folks ate. I lived through the Depression. My husband died fighting in World War II. And I lived long enough to almost become Vice-President. I seen a lot of changes in my life. I learned a few things along the way."

Her left hand was shaking, as it did sometimes if she needed to take her medication.

"One thing I learned is that life is about chances," she continued. "We only get a few good ones. When a good chance comes your way, Moon, you gotta grab it or live with the fact that you didn't."

"So you're saying I should accept the presidency?"

"You and your pal Lane did an amazing thing, winning that election. Now you got a chance. A good chance. If you don't take it, for the rest of your days you're gonna wonder what mighta happened."

"I can't be President," I said. "I don't know the first *thing* about being President. I'd be terrible. Lane and I just *tricked* America into voting for me."

"Sweetie, I lived through a lot of politicians. Very smart men. Lawyers. Governors. Senators. A lot of 'em turned out to be bums. You won't be worse. And you could be better."

"I just want to go back to being a regular kid again," I complained.

"You wanna grow up to be a trivia question?" she asked, challenging me. "Or do you wanna make a difference in the world?"

"I'm thirteen," I said, looking away from her. "What difference am *I* going to make?"

"That's up to you, Moon. The point is, you got a chance. And believe me, in the rest of your life, you're *never* gonna get another chance like this. In two hundred somethin' years, not many men have had this chance. Moon, all I'm sayin' is, you should think it over before deciding. It's not too late to change your mind."

I thought about what she had said all night long. The next morning, I called Lane.

2.
★ **First Babe** ★

"Hello?" Lane said wearily when he picked up the phone. There was music playing in the background and somebody was singing off-key.

"It's me, Moon. Who's over there?"

"The future Miss America," he moaned.

Chelsea.

Chelsea Daniels was definitely the prettiest girl in our school, maybe the prettiest girl in Wisconsin. With her impossibly long blond hair and impossibly sky blue eyes, she looked like a fashion model. In fact, she was one. After school, she modeled for some local department stores.

I didn't even *know* Chelsea when I agreed to run for President. But Lane convinced me to ask her to be my First Lady anyway. He said

I would get more votes if a gorgeous girl was on my arm. He was right. America loved Chelsea, and Chelsea loved, well . . . the attention.

When I quit the presidency, Chelsea was naturally upset that she wasn't going to be First Lady after all. She broke down crying. Lane cheered her up by telling her that she should think about entering the Miss America pageant. He promised to help her win, just as he had helped me win. Lane always likes a challenge.

"Moon!" Lane whispered into the phone. "I had no idea what I was up against! Turning Chelsea into Miss America is going to be a lot tougher than getting you elected President."

"What's the matter?"

"The girl has no talent, Moon!" he whispered. "Zero! She can't dance. She can't play a musical instrument. When she started to sing, my dog ran away. And she's dumb as a block of wood."

"Gee, I'm sorry," I said. "I'll bet she'll win the swimsuit competition, though."

I had never admitted it to Lane, but I had a secret crush on Chelsea Daniels. She was just so gorgeous! It was cool when she pretended to be my girlfriend the entire time I was running for President. I knew everybody was thinking, "This guy must be pretty special to have such a pretty girl as his First Lady."

"So what about you?" Lane asked. "How does it feel to be the first President in American history to resign before his term began?"

"Lane," I said carefully, "I changed my mind."

There was silence at the other end of the line.

"Are you there, Lane? I said I changed my mind."

"I heard you," he replied. "I was just saying a silent prayer."

"For me?"

"No, for America," Lane said. "Why do you want to do that, Moon? Quitting was the smartest thing you ever did. You get all the glory of winning the presidency without any of the hassles that come with actually being President."

"Lane, I want to do some good," I said, a bit embarrassed. "I want to make a difference."

"You want to make a difference?" Lane

laughed. "Moon, it doesn't make any difference who's President. It's all politics. Nothing ever gets done. When a Republican is President, the Democrats just trash him. When a Democrat is President, the Republicans just trash him. And because you don't belong to either party, *everybody's* going to trash you."

"I want to try, though," I pleaded. "I need you, Lane. I'll need a lot of help."

"No, Moon. I've had enough of politics."

"Let me get this straight," I said. "Instead of being the top adviser to the President of the United States, you'd rather devote your life to . . . a *beauty pageant*?"

"It's *not* a beauty pageant," Lane protested. "The girls have to be intelligent, articulate, talented —"

"Yeah, everything Chelsea is *not*. Lane, I'm giving you the chance to help me guide the United States of America! It's the chance of a lifetime."

In the background, I could hear Chelsea warbling something from *The Sound of Music*. Lane sighed. "What do you want me to do?" he asked.

"I want you to be my Secretary of State."

"The Secretary of State only handles relations with foreign countries," Lane said, which was news to me. "I'm not interested."

"Well, I want you to be whatever my closest adviser would be. My go-to guy. My right-hand man."

"That would be Chief of Staff," Lane told me.

"Then I want you to be my Chief of Staff."

Chelsea butchered "Climb Ev'ry Mountain" while Lane thought things over. I had to hold the phone away from my ear.

"Okay, I'll do it," Lane finally said.

"Great! Put Chelsea on."

I heard Lane telling Chelsea to stop singing and pick up the phone. He told her it was me, but he didn't tell her why I was calling.

"I'm not speaking to you, Judson Moon!" Chelsea shouted. "I worked my butt off helping you get elected, and how do you repay me? You resign on election night! How could you *do* that to me? Who needs you anyway, Moon? Lane is going to help me become Miss America. And I'd rather be Miss America than First Lady any day. You jerk! I hate your guts!"

"I thought you weren't speaking to me," I said quietly.

"That's all I'm going to say!"

"Chelsea, let me just say one thing," I said. "I changed my mind."

"Huh?"

"I decided to accept the presidency after all. Lane's not going to help you become Miss America. He's going to be my Chief of Staff. And if you're willing to forgive me, I'd like you to be my First Babe — I mean Lady."

Chelsea didn't say a word. Then I heard sniffling. Then crying.

"Are you okay, Chelsea?" I asked.

"This is the greatest day of my life!" she sobbed. "I'm just so *happy*! I never really wanted to be Miss America anyway."

"So you'll be First Lady?"

"Yes," Chelsea said, sniffing and pulling herself together. "But after the way you've treated me, Judson Moon, I have certain requirements that must be met."

"Requirements?

"Number one. As First Lady, I'll have to throw lots of parties," she said. "Whenever I want."

"Okay," I agreed. "That's no big deal. First Ladies entertain at the White House all the time."

"Number two," Chelsea continued, "I must have an unlimited budget for clothing, cosmetics, and hairstyling."

"Uh, ask Lane how much the President gets paid," I instructed her.

"Four hundred thousand dollars a year," she reported back a few seconds later.

"Whew!" I whistled. "Okay, you can have as much money as you need. The First Lady has to look her best, I guess."

"Number three. You must agree *never* to ask me out on a date or try to kiss me or anything."

"What makes you think I would ask you out or kiss you?" I replied.

"*All* boys want to ask me out and kiss me."

"I promise I won't ask you out or try to kiss you," I agreed.

"Good," Chelsea said happily. "As long as we're in agreement. So when is Inauguration Day, Moon?"

"January twentieth."

"That's only five weeks away!" she said in a panic. "I've got to go!"

"Why?"

"To pick out my dress, silly! I don't have a *thing* to wear!"

3.
★ Let's Make a Deal ★

The weatherman had predicted rain in the Washington, D.C., area for Inauguration Day, but as I mounted the podium on the west side of the Capitol Building, the clouds parted to reveal a beautiful sunny but chilly January day.

As I looked out across the National Mall, I was struck most of all by the people. Thousands and thousands had jammed the grassy area outside the Smithsonian museums that line both sides of the Mall. They spilled out onto Independence Avenue and Pennsylvania Avenue. The sea of faces stretched all the way to the Washington Monument off in the distance.

Flags were everywhere. Enormous ones flying from every building and tiny ones in the hands of little children. Marching bands played enthusiastically. "Yankee Doodle." "The Battle Hymn of the Republic."

As I turned to look at the stands behind the podium, I spotted my mom and dad beaming at me and waving. I wasn't sure how they were going to deal with me being President. All my life they had been in charge of me. Now I would be in charge of . . . *everyone.*

My parents were standing next to Chelsea Daniels — dressed to kill, of course — and her parents.

Mrs. Syers was sitting in her wheelchair behind me, her hands folded in her lap, looking very regal and proud. She had already been sworn in as Vice-President.

Lane was up in the stands in a corner seat, with a smirk on his face. I wouldn't have been able to get elected president of the student council at school without him, and he knew it.

The rest of the bleachers was filled with dignitaries — senators, members of Congress, Supreme Court justices, the outgoing President, and all the living ex-Presidents.

At precisely noon, the Chief Justice of the

Supreme Court leaned into his microphone and asked, "Mr. Moon, are you prepared to take the oath of office as President of the United States?"

"I am, sir."

The Chief Justice held up a Bible, the same one George Washington had used when he was sworn in as our country's first President back in 1789. Shivers went up and down my spine as I raised my right hand and repeated those thirty-seven words that change history:

> "I, Judson Moon, do solemnly swear that I will faithfully execute the Office of President of the United States, and will, to the best of my ability, preserve, protect, and defend the Constitution of the United States."

I wasn't old enough to vote. I couldn't legally drive a car. I couldn't take a sip of my dad's beer. But I was President of the United States. I felt like I had to be in the middle of a dream. It couldn't really be happening.

Only in America!

A twenty-one-gun salute echoed off the buildings and a cheer went up from the crowd. Balloons rose into the air. Doves were released. The Marine Band played "Hail to the Chief."

The former President, who was now just an ordinary citizen, shook my hand. "Good Luck, President Moon," he said solemnly as he handed me a large brown briefcase. "This is for you. Take good care of it, young man."

Nobody had told me the President was going to give me a *gift*. Considering that I had beaten him in the election, it was very gracious of him. I didn't really like the color of the briefcase, but my mother always told me that when someone gave me a gift I should pretend I loved it, whether I really liked it or not.

"Thank you, Mr. President," I said. "I can hardly wait to use it."

The President looked horrified. The Chief Justice leaned over and whispered into my ear.

"That briefcase," he said, "contains the instructions for launching nuclear missiles in case there is an attack on the United States. Keep it by your side always."

Oops! One minute into my presidency and I

had already goofed! I leaned back to the former President and told him that I hoped I would never have to use his "gift."

When the crowd settled down and everyone in the stands took their seats, I stepped up to the microphone. Lane had worked hard on my Inaugural Address.

"My fellow Americans," I said, hearing the words echo a second after I spoke them. "When I was running for President, I said you should vote for me because I didn't know anything about politics. I didn't know how to raise taxes. I didn't know how to ruin the economy. I didn't know how to get us into a war. I said you should vote for me because I didn't know *anything*."

The crowd chuckled in appreciation.

"Well, that was two months ago, and I'm very proud to say that . . . (Lane told me to pause here) I *still* don't know anything!"

The crowd roared in approval.

"Let's face it," I continued, "I'm a kid. I'm going to need a lot of help from all of you. Kids and grown-ups. Men and women. Rich and poor. People of all races. Will you help me?"

"Yessssssssssssssssssss!" the crowd thundered.

"My fellow Americans. President Theodore Roosevelt gave the country what he called a Square Deal. President Franklin D. Roosevelt gave the country a New Deal. President Truman gave us a Fair Deal. Today I say this to America — Let's make a deal."

Everybody went nuts.

"Here's the deal I offer America — I'll help you all if you all help me. I'm not a Republican, so you Democrats have no reason to oppose me. I'm not a Democrat, so you Republicans have no reason to oppose me. But if we all work together, we can guide our nation together."

There was too much applause to continue, so I let it die down until everybody could hear me.

"Together, we can clean up the environment," I announced. "Together, we can educate children and take care of our senior citizens. Together, we can put an *end* to crime, an *end* to poverty, an *end* to unemployment, an *end* to inflation, an *end* to peace in the world."

There was a gasp. I looked at my speech and saw that I had skipped a line.

"I mean, we're going to *have* peace in the world."

A thunderous ovation rolled across the Mall.

"The twentieth century is over, the twenty-first has begun. We've got a lot of work to do. So, America, I ask you, ARE YOU READY TO RUMMMMMBLE?"

"Yeahhhhhhhhhhhh!"

"Let's get it on," I concluded.

They didn't stop applauding for twenty minutes.

Somebody ushered me into a ridiculously long limousine for the parade down Pennsylvania Avenue, which leads directly from the Capitol to the White House. My mom and dad were already inside the car.

"Great speech, sweetie!" Mom said, giving me a hug.

"Except for that part about ending world peace," grumbled Dad.

I looked through the window as the limo pulled away. There were people everywhere. Military men in uniform saluted as I passed by.

Kids had climbed trees along the route to get a look at me. I waved, and so did Mom and Dad. Their pictures had been all over the media, so just about everybody recognized them.

At 14th Street, a few blocks from the White House, I could hear people chanting, "Walk! Walk! Walk!"

Lane had told me that in recent years the new President usually got out of the limousine at some point and walked part of the way along the parade route.

I was prepared. I leaned down, took off my shoes, and pulled on my Rollerblades.

"You're not really going to put those silly things on, are you?" my dad asked.

"I sure am, Dad."

"It's not dignified for the President of the United States to roller-skate down the street," Dad complained. "I forbid you to do it."

"Who's the President, Dad?" I asked as I tightened the laces. "You or me?"

Dad looked stunned. I had never spoken to him like that. But this was *my* day, and I wasn't going to let my parents ruin it.

The crowd roared when I hopped out of the limo and glided onto the pavement. Five or six Secret Service agents, who were in the car behind mine, quickly jumped out and jogged after me nervously.

The cool breeze felt great. I waved to everybody. I couldn't resist hamming it up a bit. I grabbed the back bumper of the limo and let it pull me down the street. I skated backward and waved to the people behind me. I skated over to the line of people at the curb and put out my hand for them to slap. Then I circled back and did the same thing with the people on the other side of the street. I was having a ball.

Soon, the White House came into view. I had seen pictures of the building, but I'd never been there. Up close, it was even bigger and more beautiful than I had imagined.

A bunch of soldiers with rifles saluted me and I saluted them back. The President, Lane had reminded me, is the Commander in Chief of the Armed Forces. The soldiers led me up the East Gate steps. The huge front door opened. A very distinguished-looking elderly gentleman with perfectly combed white hair and a dark suit stood at attention.

"President Moon," he said with a bow, "welcome to your new home."

4.
★ Nice Place ★

The sweet old man who greeted me at the door of the White House introduced himself as Roger Honeywell. He said he was the Chief Usher of the White House. When I asked him what that meant, he said he did a "little bit of this and a little bit of that" to keep the household running.

Essentially, he told me, he was the President's butler and servant. That sounded pretty cool to me. I always thought it would be great to have a servant.

Honeywell had been working at the White House for many years, he told me. He was about as old as Vice-President Syers and maybe even older. It wouldn't have surprised me if he greeted George Washington after *his* inauguration.

"My only purpose, Mr. President, is to make you, your family, and your guests happy."

"You need to get a life," I told Honeywell.

"I beg your pardon, sir?" he asked. "My hearing isn't what it once was."

"He said you need to get a *wife*."

The voice came from Vice-President Syers, who had wheeled herself up the ramp ahead of my parents. Mrs. Syers would be living in the Vice-President's mansion a few miles away in northwest Washington, but she wanted to tour the White House as much as any of us.

"Perhaps I *will* get married someday," Honeywell sighed, "if the right woman ever comes along."

"She better hurry up," I said.

"I beg your pardon, President Moon?"

"He said we better hurry up," corrected Vice-President Syers, shooting me a stern look I hadn't seen since she was my baby-sitter so long ago.

My parents arrived and then Chelsea Daniels and her parents finally made their way up the front steps. Chelsea had stopped to pose for some photographers outside the East Gate.

"Nice place," my dad muttered. That was high praise, coming from my dad. He doesn't usually approve of anything.

"It's lovely," Mom gushed. Mom thinks everything is lovely.

"If everyone is here, we'd better get going," Honeywell announced. "The White House has a hundred and thirty-two rooms and you'll want to see them all."

Honeywell grabbed Vice-President Syers' wheelchair and began to push it. He led us through the first floor, which he called the State Floor. This is where the President entertains guests. It's the only part of the building tourists are allowed to visit.

"George Washington was the only President who didn't live in the White House," Honeywell informed us as he led us into the Blue Room. "It was being built when he was President."

The Blue Room was oval and decorated with long blue drapes. "The President greets guests here," Honeywell said. "The seven gilded Bellangé chairs were ordered from France by Monroe."

"Marilyn Monroe?" I marveled.

"*James* Monroe, sir," Honeywell replied dryly. "Our fifth President. Though I understand Miss Monroe did visit the White House on several occasions."

"The chairs are lovely," my mom said.

"I might have them reupholstered," Chelsea mused.

Honeywell led us into the Red Room next. "This is a sitting room," he said. "That's Scalamandré silk. Harrison put it in."

"George Harrison?" I asked. "The Beatle?"

"*William Henry* Harrison, sir," Honeywell corrected. "Our ninth President. But George Harrison also visited the White House, when President Ford lived here."

The Green Room was next, decorated with green silk on the walls. Honeywell said that Garfield put it in.

"Garfield the cat?" I asked.

"*James* Garfield, sir," he replied. "Our twentieth President."

"Just busting your chops," I whispered to Honeywell.

In all these rooms, portraits of past Presidents covered the walls. I recognized a lot of them from school. Some of them weren't familiar.

"Who's that, Honeywell?" I asked.

"Rutherford B. Hayes," he replied. "He was the first President to speak on the telephone."

"What did he say?" I asked.

"What?" replied Honeywell.

"What were his first words on the phone, Honeywell?"

"What. He said what, sir."

"On the *phone*," I demanded. "What were his first words?"

"What, President Moon."

"Forget it," I said disgustedly.

"That was the *second* thing he said," Honeywell informed us. Then he leaned over to me and whispered, "Just busting your chops, Mr. President."

An eighty-year-old guy who still busts chops is okay by me, I decided.

There were two enormous rooms on the State Floor — the East Room and the State Dining Room. Both had floor-to-ceiling windows, fireplaces in all the corners, and enormous chandeliers. Honeywell told us the two rooms were used for receptions, balls, and press conferences. I couldn't help but notice that either room would be just the right size for a basketball court.

"I can throw the most divine parties here!" Chelsea gushed.

As we walked around, I noticed that there were clusters of people standing around, bowing and smiling politely.

"Are these people *always* here?" I asked Honeywell.

"The White House has almost a hundred employees," he informed me. "Ushers, maids, butlers, cooks, waiters, window washers. Every piece of furniture gets polished daily."

"What do *you* do?" I asked a guy in a military uniform who was holding an American flag.

"I carry a flag around and put it behind you, Mr. President."

"What for?"

"So every photo of you has a flag in it, sir."

"What's *your* job?" I asked a lady.

"I clean the toilets, Mr. President," she replied. "There are thirty-two of them in the White House."

"And they say the *President's* job is tough!" I cracked. "And what do *you* do?" I asked a man my father's age.

"I'm the new food taster, Mr. President," he said. "I taste all your food to make sure it hasn't been poisoned."

"Where's the old food taster?"

"He died, sir."

"Died?!"

"From natural causes, Mr. President."

"Well, that's good," I said before asking another lady what she did.

"I'm a secretary," she said.

"Whose secretary?" I asked.

"The Secretary of Defense."

"The Secretary of Defense has a secretary?"

"Oh yes, sir," she replied. "And so do I."

"So your secretary is the Secretary of Defense's secretary's secretary?"

"Yes, sir."

Honeywell led us to an elevator, which took us down to the White House basement. There, we saw a barbershop, a doctor's office, a machine shop, a plumber's shop, and a kitchen with a refrigerator so big that you could walk into it. I had no idea the White House had all this stuff in it.

Also downstairs was the Map Room. There are enormous maps on the walls. Honeywell told us that this is where President Franklin D. Roosevelt followed the progress of our troops in World War II.

We all got back into the elevator, which took us up to the second floor. That's where the President's living quarters are. Between my family and Chelsea's family, we would fill every bedroom on the second floor except for one. Honeywell saved that one for last.

"And this is the Lincoln Bedroom," he said reverently as he opened the door.

The room was decorated simply, with just a small desk and a bed. The bed was huge, maybe eight feet long.

"Lincoln was our tallest President," Honeywell told us. "Six feet four inches."

"The bed is lumpy," muttered my dad.

"Even so, it's lovely," Mom insisted.

"Actually, Lincoln never slept in this bed,"

Honeywell claimed. "It was being built for him when he was assassinated. But he was embalmed in this room."

"Creepy," Chelsea said. "That desk has got to go. It's hideous."

"With all due respect, Miss Daniels, I believe the desk belongs here."

"Why?"

"Lincoln signed the Emancipation Proclamation on it — the document that put an end to slavery in this country."

That shut Chelsea up. I noticed that a framed copy of the Gettysburg Address on the wall was slightly crooked. I went over and straightened it.

"I guess he's been here again," Honeywell sighed.

"Who?" Vice-President Syers asked.

"Abraham Lincoln," Honeywell said in a hushed voice. "The President's ghost, some believe, lives in this room. Teddy Roosevelt claimed he saw it. So did Queen Wilhelmina of the Netherlands. And President Eisenhower said he sensed its presence."

"That's spooky," Chelsea said. "Let's get out of here."

Up on the third floor, Honeywell showed us the White House laundry, servants' rooms, dental clinic, tailor shop, carpentry shop, sun room, guest bedrooms, and what was sure to be Chelsea's favorite room — the beauty salon. By the time we got back on the elevator, everybody was exhausted.

"Oh, I almost forgot," Honeywell said, lurching for the second-floor button as the elevator made its way down. He led us to the West Wing of the White House and opened the door to a room he hadn't shown us earlier.

"This," he said dramatically, "is the Oval Office."

I was almost afraid to go inside. The Oval Office is the working office of the President of the United States. Lincoln had used this room. Kennedy. The Roosevelts. All the Presidents since Washington. It was in this room that Presidents struggled with decisions that changed the course of history. I was in awe.

"Go ahead, Moon," Mrs. Syers urged me. "Sit in the chair. See how it feels."

Hesitantly, I Rollerbladed around the big wooden desk, which was flanked by flags and large potted plants. There was a huge blue rug on the floor with the seal of the President of the United States in the middle of it.

I gazed out the window. The Washington Monument was straight ahead. I sank into the big chair and looked at everybody.

"He's not my little boy anymore," my mom said, sniffling like she was about to cry.

"Lookin' good," Mrs. Syers said, beaming. "You da man, Moon. The most powerful man on the planet."

"Actually, there is *one* person who can tell the President where to go and what to do."

"Who's that?" I asked.

"He's waiting outside," said Honeywell.

5.
Secret Service Agent
★ John Doe ★

The door to the Oval Office opened. In walked a guy who I can only describe as a giant slab of beef with a head on top. He was an enormous bald-headed African-American man with posture so straight, he must have had a steel bar running up and down his back. Three hundred pounds, easy. He was wearing a blue blazer and carrying a large cardboard box, which he put on a shelf. He looked to be in his forties.

This monster of a man marched stiffly toward me, saluted crisply, and stuck out his hand. I shook it. Or, to be more accurate, it shook *me*. His hand was about the size of a catcher's mitt.

"Secret Service Agent John Doe, sir," he said in a quick, clipped voice. "Presidential Protection Division."

"John Doe?" I asked. "That's not your *real* name, is it?"

"Yes it is, sir."

"Come on," I kidded him. "The Secret Service just *gave* you that name for security reasons, right?"

"No, Mr. President, John Doe is my real name."

"You're not even allowed to reveal your real name to the President, are you?"

"Sir, I am duty-bound not to lie. John Doe is my real name."

"Your parents couldn't think of anything else?"

"They considered many alternatives, sir. Decided they liked John Doe best."

"Well, if they like it, I like it, too."

"Thank you, sir. I'm going to have to ask Chief Usher Honeywell and your family to exit the Oval Office at this time, sir. Vice-President Syers, too. Security, you understand."

Honeywell escorted everyone out of the Oval Office and shut the door behind him. Agent Doe and I were alone.

"You look like you must have been a football player, Agent Doe."

"Never played the game, sir. Decided it wasn't physical enough, sir."

"Is that a joke?" I asked.

"I never joke, sir."

"Do you end every statement with the word sir?"

"Usually, sir."

"Do you ever smile?"

"Rarely, sir."

I made a mental note. If I could make this guy laugh — just once — my presidency would be a success.

"Maybe you should relax a little," I suggested. "Being so stiff like that can't be good for you. Lighten up. Have a little fun."

"Not advisable, sir," he replied. "For the next four years, I have one specific goal — keeping you alive, sir."

"Do you really think somebody would try to hurt me?" I asked.

"Sir, the Secret Service has files on hundreds of individuals who have made threats against

41

the President. Some people will disagree with your policies enough to want you dead. Others are mentally unbalanced. Some just think they will become famous by killing you."

"I'm not worried," I laughed.

"Sir, four of our Presidents — Lincoln, Garfield, McKinley, and Kennedy — were assassinated. Attempts were made on the lives of several others."

"If anybody tries to kill me, I'll just hide behind *you*," I joked.

"That's why I'm here, sir. Actually, the Secret Service is more concerned about kidnapping. If somebody were to kidnap the President or a member of his family, it would bring the United States to its knees. Cannot be too cautious, sir. You'll need to listen carefully to everything I say for your protection and the protection of the nation."

"I understand."

"Whenever you leave the White House, you will be accompanied by myself and about ten other agents. In public, when people put out their hands to shake, it is important that you just *touch* hands with them, sir. Don't clasp."

"Why not?"

"Someone could grab you and pull you into the crowd, sir. Very dangerous."

"Okay."

"Do not accept *anything* that anybody hands you in a crowd, sir. I don't care if it's a teddy bear. Don't take it."

"It could be a bomb, huh?" I guessed. "An exploding teddy bear?"

"Right. Move through crowds as quickly as possible. If you're a target, be a moving target. See this window behind your desk? Don't stand in front of it. A sharpshooter perched on the roof of that building across the street would be within firing range."

"Wow," I said, peeking through the curtains.

"Sir, you should be aware that outside the White House are a series of five-thousand-pound concrete barriers that should stop any suicide truck bomb. If they don't, the White House is surrounded by an eight-foot iron fence. The gates are crashproof. If an enemy somehow made it past the fence, there are pressure sensors on the lawn. Ground-to-air missiles are hidden nearby. If we give the order, the missiles will be launched and will destroy a tank. We also have dogs that sniff for explosives. And all guests entering the White House must pass through a metal detector."

"Is that it?" I asked.

"No, sir. If an enemy submarine was hidden off the East Coast, it could launch a nuclear missile that would level Washington in six to eight minutes. We have satellites orbiting hundreds of miles above the earth with cameras so powerful they can photograph objects on the ground the size of a large horse. If our satellites detect missiles heading for the White House, you will be led to the bomb shelter in the basement under the East Wing."

"What if somebody attacks on very small horses?" I quipped, trying to get Agent Doe to laugh. He didn't.

"Missiles are more likely, sir. If there is time, you will be evacuated. We will get you to a 747 jet at Andrews Air Force Base that has been specially reinforced to absorb the heat and impact of a nuclear blast. It is on alert twenty-four hours a day. In the event of a nuclear war, it will serve as the temporary headquarters of our government."

"So I could watch as Washington gets blown to bits?"

"No, sir," Agent Doe replied. "The plane has no windows."

He pointed to a red telephone on the desk.

"Sir, this telephone is the hot line. It is a two-way system that links the White House and the Kremlin in Moscow. If there is an international crisis, the leaders of both the United States and Russia can communicate directly. You do not have to dial. Just pick up the receiver and there is an instant connection. Hopefully, this will reduce the risk of war because of a misunderstanding. Any questions, sir?"

"Do you carry a gun?" I asked.

"Certainly, sir."

"Did you ever shoot anyone?"

"I have never fired my weapon, no, sir."

"Do you know jujitsu and kung fu and stuff?"

"Yes, sir."

"Could you, like, paralyze a guy in ten seconds?"

"Three seconds, sir, if necessary."

"Wow! You have the coolest job in the world."

"Some would say the same of you, sir."

"Can you show me how to do that? Paralyze a guy in three seconds?"

"I will have to check regulations, sir, to see if that is allowed. Right now, there is one more thing to go over. I have to show you how to use the football. Where is it?"

"Football?" I asked. "What football?"

"The football," he said, his voice rising with urgency. "The brown briefcase you were handed right after you were sworn in. We call that the football."

"Oh yeah!" I recalled. "The briefcase. The President gave it to me."

"Where is it, sir?"

"I, uh . . . guess I left it at the podium."

Agent Doe grabbed for his walkie-talkie like he was reaching for his gun.

"Code red!" he barked. "Repeat! Code red! We have a fumble situation! Repeat! Fumble situation! Live ball near podium at Capitol Building! Code red! Return immediately! Urgent!"

Instantly, a siren went off outside. A bunch of cars gunned their engines and screeched away. Agent Doe spat out a curse word in his disgust and immediately apologized to me.

"I'll go back and get it!" I said frantically. "I can Rollerblade over there in a minute."

"You're not to leave this room!" Agent Doe warned forcefully. "This is a matter of national security, sir. If the football has fallen into the wrong hands, you will be needed here."

"What do you mean by the wrong hands?" I asked.

"Terrorists, sir. Mentally disturbed persons. Unfriendly governments."

"I'm sorry!" I moaned. "Oh man, I messed up big time! How could I have been so stupid?"

"What's done is done, sir," Agent Doe said. "Let's just hope our team can recover the fumble."

I sat there sweating for a few minutes as the siren got farther away. Any idiot on the street could have picked up the suitcase and launched a bunch of nukes for the fun of it. Millions of people could die. I couldn't breathe. Agent Doe paced back and forth. He wouldn't look at me. I was afraid to look at him. Then his walkie-talkie beeped and he had it on his ear in a flash.

"Fumble recovered!" he shouted excitedly.

I exhaled.

"A janitor found it behind the podium, sir, and turned it over to the police."

"We should give him a medal or something," I suggested.

"Wouldn't advise that course of action, sir. Better to keep this incident quiet. If word gets out that you misplaced the football, it will make you look bad. Nasty headlines have ended more presidencies than bullets."

In seconds, another Secret Service agent entered the Oval Office, carrying the brown briefcase. He handed it to me, saluted, and left without saying a word.

"This is of vital importance, sir," Agent Doe said, staring intently at me. "The football must be with you *at all times*. It must go with you *everywhere*. It must be with you when you eat, when you sleep."

"I won't let it out of my sight," I promised.

"Good," Agent Doe said as he moved toward

the doorway. "It has been a long day for you, sir, and you have a busy night ahead of you. I'm going to leave you alone now. I will be right outside the door if you need anything."

"Thank you, Agent Doe."

"Oh," he said, picking up the box he had left on the shelf. "This is for you."

"You didn't have to get me a gift!" I said, embarrassed.

"It's from the Defense Department, sir," he said. "Bulletproof clothing."

"I've got to wear bulletproof clothes?" I asked, opening the box. The suit inside looked like a regular men's suit but heavier and stiffer.

"It would be advisable, sir, for your protection."

"Bulletproof *underwear*?" I asked, holding up a pair of briefs. "Do you really think some lunatic's going to try and shoot me in the butt?"

"They'll probably try to shoot you in the head," he replied. "But they might miss and hit you in the butt, sir."

The things a guy's gotta do for his country! I thanked Agent Doe and walked him to the door.

"Agent Doe," I said, putting out my hand

again to shake, "what do you think would have happened if the football fell into the wrong hands?"

"Sir, there are enough nuclear weapons in the world to incinerate it and leave it uninhabitable. Right now, half the planet could have been destroyed. Man has the power to destroy mankind."

"Thank you, Agent Doe."

"You're welcome, President Moon."

I was exhausted, but my day wasn't over yet. On the evening of the inauguration the new President and First Lady have to attend a ball. When I knocked on Chelsea's door wearing sweatpants and a T-shirt, she almost fainted.

"You're supposed to wear a tuxedo, Moon!" she shouted. "It's a ball, not a ball game!"

"I don't have a tuxedo," I explained.

I went back to my room and put on a suit I had gotten for a friend's confirmation last year. It didn't fit that well, but it was okay.

It turned out that it wasn't *one* ball I had to go to but twelve! Basically, they were fancy dinner parties where rich and powerful people get to dress up and hang out with other rich and powerful people. Chelsea and I would enter the ball arm in arm, say hello to everybody for five minutes, and then get back into the limo and go to the next ball. By the second ball, I was sick of it.

Chelsea loved every second, though. She looked great. Lane told me Chelsea had spent $10,000 on her gown. That was hard to believe. Chelsea hadn't given me the bill yet, so I couldn't say for sure. I didn't even know you could *find* a dress that cost so much money.

When I finally got back to the White House, I was so tired I didn't even put my pajamas on. I just lay on my bed in my suit and fell asleep.

6.
★ Class Trip ★

Chief of Staff Lane Brainard made it a point to stay out of the way during the inauguration and tour of the White House. He told me he didn't want to be seen with me all the time, because people would get the impression that *he* was really running everything.

Of course, we both knew that Lane really *would* be running everything. What did I know about being President?

Lane told me to enjoy my first weekend as President, because starting Monday morning, we would have to get to work running the country.

I thought about it and decided the best way to really enjoy the weekend would be to invite my seventh-grade class to the White House. No parents, just kids. Chief Usher Honeywell called all twenty-four kids personally, and every one of them accepted the invitation. I sent my parents off on a tour of Washington to keep them out of the way. Chelsea Daniels decided she'd rather go shopping with her parents than hang out with us kids.

At first, my classmates were a little shy about being in the White House for the first time. They were afraid to touch anything or sit on the chairs. With Secret Service Agent Doe always nearby and Honeywell hovering around, I could understand the kids being a little nervous.

I explained that the White House was my home, at least for four years, and they could treat it just like they were going over to anybody else's house.

Everybody loosened up when I showed them all the cool stuff around the White House. On the South Lawn is a tennis court that's surrounded by trees so people on the street can't gawk. Erica McCabe and Athena Theodoris love tennis, so even though it was cold they grabbed rackets and began to play.

I took the rest of the class to the White House

bowling alley, which is under the driveway. President Nixon bowled a 233 there once, Honeywell told us. Gillian Dougherty and Meaghan Delaney are in a bowling league back home, so they decided to roll a game.

The rest of us went to the White House game room, where there's a pool table, a Ping-Pong table, and some video games. Kids started peeling off from the group to play whatever they wanted. Video games are my passion, but I wanted to show everyone around, so I didn't get a chance to play.

There are television sets all over the White House, and some of the rooms have five or six TV's lined up together so the President can watch the news on all the major networks at the same time. Anne Maloney turned on a roomful of TV's, putting one on MTV, one on the Cartoon Network, one on Nickelodeon, one on ESPN, and one on Fox. A bunch of us gathered to watch all the TV's at once, with the sound turned all the way up. After a half hour, our heads felt like they were splitting open, but it was great fun.

Maybe the coolest thing about living in the White House is that it's got its own movie theater. There are sixty-five seats, and cushy reclining chairs line the front row.

"What movies do you have?" I asked Honeywell.

"I can get any movie you want, sir. Even movies that haven't been released yet."

"How about *Gore, Guts, and Guns, Part II*?" I asked.

"I don't believe I've heard of that one," Honeywell replied.

"It comes out next month," I informed him. "I saw the preview on *Entertainment Tonight*."

"I'll see if I can track it down, sir," Honeywell said, and he went trotting off. I was beginning to appreciate the power of the presidency.

With Honeywell out of the way for a while, my classmates started getting goofy. Things started to get out of control. Sarah Godlewski and Erica Johnson had a skateboard race around the East Room, knocking over Woodrow Wilson's candlesticks. Alexandra Edwards and John Nosek went up on the roof of the White House and dropped water balloons on the Secret Service agents stationed outside. Aaron Taylor dumped pepper into a bag of Cheez Doodles and we had my food taster eat them to make sure they weren't poisoned. Somebody scribbled MILLARD FILLMORE WAS A DORK with a bar of soap on a bathroom mirror.

When Honeywell came back and saw what was going on, he looked a little frazzled, but he didn't yell at us or anything. I don't think he was allowed to. He politely whispered to me that perhaps my friends could burn off some of their extra energy if they went for a swim. It sounded like a great idea.

There's an underground tunnel that leads from the White House to a big pool not far from the Oval Office. It was freezing outside, but the pool was heated and most of the kids couldn't resist jumping in.

Agent Doe stood at the side of the pool, keeping an eye on things, I guess to make sure none of the kids tried to dunk me or anything.

"Come on in, Agent Doe," I called. "The water's fine!"

"No thank you, sir," he replied.

"Hey, Mr. Secret Service Man," Luke Peyton called, "can I shoot your gun?"

"No."

"Hey, Moon!" Stephen Cohn shouted. "Why don't you put on your bulletproof underwear and we'll take turns shooting you in the butt?"

"Not a good idea," Agent Doe said seriously. I had made the mistake of telling my classmates about the underwear.

"Hey, if one of us attacked Moon," asked Emily Mulholland, "would you kill us?"

"No, I would just render you unconscious."

"Can you do that to our teacher?" asked Emma Samuels.

We were all having a great time. Even Agent Doe seemed to enjoy the wisecracks.

I didn't notice that a bunch of the boys had climbed out of the pool and snuck around behind Agent Doe. He didn't notice, either, because he was watching me. It wasn't until they were running toward him that I saw them out the corner of my eye.

"No!" I screamed. "Don't!"

It was too late. The boys rammed into him at full speed and Agent Doe toppled over. He hit the water like a bomb. I actually felt the water level in the pool go up a little because his body took up so much space.

Everybody thought it was the funniest thing they'd ever seen. I did, too, until I noticed that Agent Doe was flailing his arms around and struggling to keep his head above water.

"He can't swim!" I shouted.

"Somebody rescue him!" Molly Lenny yelled.

"I can't rescue him," hollered Christine Marcozzi. "He's too big!"

"We can't just leave him there!" screamed Chloe Shean. "He'll drown!"

Agent Doe was going underwater for the second time. While everybody stood around arguing, I swam over to him and grabbed him around the neck. It was hard to do, because his neck was about as thick as my waist. But I had taken a lifesaving course at summer camp one year, and I knew the basics of how to handle somebody who was drowning.

I got Agent Doe's head out of the water and slowly began pulling him to the shallow end of the pool. It was like dragging a whale ashore.

It took six of us to haul him out of the water and lay him down on the concrete. He was gasping for air and his walkie-talkie was ruined, but it looked like he was going to make it.

"Are you okay, Doe?" I asked.

"I think so," he choked, spitting out water. "I thought I was supposed to protect *your* life, sir, not the other way around."

After that fiasco, I thought it would be a good idea to get the kids out of the pool area. It was almost dinnertime anyway. When everyone was dried off and dressed, I took them up to the Oval Office. The kids were really impressed. Most of them wanted to sit in my chair and have their picture taken.

"I'm starving," Luke Peyton said as he sat at my desk. "What's for dinner?"

"Anything you want," I replied. "This is the White House."

"Pizza!" everybody yelled at once.

"We have to have it delivered," I told them.

"Cool," Luke said. Before I could stop him, he picked up the receiver of the red phone on the desk.

"No!" I shouted.

"What's the matter, Moon?"

"That's the hot line!"

"You've got a hot line to the pizza parlor?"

Luke marveled. "Man, being President is the coolest."

Somebody in Russia must have picked up at the other end. Luke looked puzzled, like he couldn't understand what the person was saying.

"Do you speak English?" Luke asked. "We want four large pies with everything on 'em. Delivered to the White House."

There was a long pause. We all stared at Luke when he put down the receiver.

"What did they say?" I asked nervously.

"Call Pizza Hut," Luke said calmly.

So we did.

After dinner, Honeywell told me he had a big surprise. He led a brown-haired guy over to me. The guy was holding one of those metal film cans that are nearly the size of a manhole cover.

"President Moon, I'd like to introduce you to Mr. Robert Banks."

"Rob Banks!" I shouted excitedly. "The guy who directed *Gore, Guts, and Guns*! I love your movies! You came all the way from Hollywood to see me?"

"I was in New York when they tracked me down, Mr. President," Rob Banks said. "I heard you wanted to see my next movie. It's not quite finished yet, but I brought along what I've got so far."

We all went to the White House movie theater. Honeywell fired up the popcorn machine and we watched the new movie along with Rob Banks. It was great.

"Those explosions were awesome," I told Mr. Banks when the lights came back on. "I love watching stuff blow up."

"Who doesn't?" Rob Banks replied with a laugh.

"You should make a whole movie with nothing but stuff blowing up," I suggested.

"That's not a bad idea, Mr. President," he said as he shook my hand.

That's one of the best things about being President, I discovered. People say your ideas are great no matter how stupid your ideas are.

After the movie, Rob Banks left and all the kids sat around the Lincoln Bedroom talking about the great day we had. We were hoping the ghost of Abraham Lincoln might appear. He never showed up, so we went to bed.

On Sunday, we had another blast. Honeywell, probably to get us out of the White House before we completely wrecked the place, suggested I take my classmates to Camp David.

Camp David is a presidential retreat sixty miles from Washington in the mountains of Maryland. President Eisenhower named it after his grandson. Presidents go there when they need some peace and quiet. We all piled into helicopters, and twenty-five minutes later we were there.

I was afraid that Camp David would be a big bore, but it was almost like Disney World. There's a heated pool, horses, snowmobiles, a golf course, a skeet and archery range, and a badminton court.

It even has a trampoline. It was hard to imagine Richard Nixon bouncing around on a trampoline, but *I* sure enjoyed it. We all had a wonderful time.

When we got back to the White House on Sunday night, another surprise was awaiting us. Earlier that morning, Honeywell had told me that many actors and musicians had visited the White House and performed there. All the President has to do is ask, he said, and celebrities are usually thrilled to be invited.

Honeywell mentioned that the Juilliard String Quartet happened to be in Washington that weekend, and maybe they would perform for me and my friends. I asked him if anyone else was in town. He looked into it and said he could get either the New York Harp Ensemble or a Suzuki violin group.

"Do you think you can get Aerosmith?" I requested.

"I'm not familiar with him, sir."

"It's a quintet," I informed him. "Very classical. They've been performing together for thirty years. Really excellent."

No way I was going to tell Honeywell that Aerosmith was the loudest, raunchiest, and most outrageous rock-and-roll band in history.

But Honeywell got on the phone, and when we returned from Camp David, Aerosmith's lead singer, Steven Tyler, was in the Blue Room, drinking champagne out of one of Thomas Jefferson's crystal goblets!

Wow! I got to meet the guys in the band, and they even asked for *my* autograph.

We gathered my classmates in the State Dining Room, and Aerosmith put on a show that just knocked our socks off. My ears were ringing, the walls were shaking, and I was seriously afraid that the giant chandeliers hanging from the ceiling were going to come crashing down on everybody. If Honeywell hadn't been hard of hearing, I think he would have run screaming out of the place.

For their encore, Steven Tyler and Joe Perry hauled me up onto the stage to sing "Walk This Way" with them. It was the greatest moment of my life.

I felt sad when all the kids said their goodbyes and piled into limos to go to the airport and fly back to Wisconsin. The White House seemed so quiet suddenly. I almost wished I could go with them.

Honeywell came over to me when the last limo pulled away. He looked exhausted. Wordlessly, he handed me *The Washington Post*.

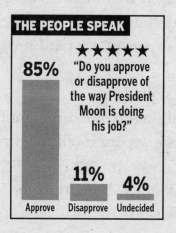

THE PEOPLE SPEAK

85% Approve

★★★★★ "Do you approve or disapprove of the way President Moon is doing his job?"

11% Disapprove

4% Undecided

"It looks like you're doing a great job, sir," Honeywell said. "In all my years at the White House, I have never seen such a high approval rating."

"But I haven't *done* anything yet!" I complained.

"You apparently do nothing rather well," Honeywell said. Then he handed me a piece of paper. It was a bill — for ten thousand dollars.

"What's this for?" I asked.

"Food, helicopters, limousines, taxis, telephone calls . . ."

"You mean the President has to *pay* for all that?" I assumed that the President didn't have to pay for anything.

"Personal expenses are paid for by the President, sir."

"Pay it," I sighed.

Honeywell then handed me another piece of paper. It was a separate bill for three thousand dollars.

"The First Lady bought some clothes this weekend," he said.

It cost a fortune to be President, I realized. But thinking it over, it was worth it. I had just enjoyed the greatest weekend of my life. Being President of the United States was *fun*!

7.
The American
★ Way of Life ★

After my friends left the White House on Sunday night, I couldn't sleep. I kept thinking about all the fun we had. Usually when I can't sleep, I pace. I started walking up and down the long hall that runs the length of the second floor.

As I passed the Lincoln Bedroom, I heard a noise. It sounded like papers rustling. I stopped in my tracks to listen. Yes, it was definitely coming from the Lincoln Bedroom. Somebody was in there!

Lincoln! It had to be the ghost of Abraham Lincoln! Everybody was asleep. Lincoln's ghost supposedly lived in the Lincoln Bedroom and came out from time to time. I was frightened, but I wanted to see him for myself.

Slowly, I turned the doorknob. Hesitantly, I opened the door a crack and peeked inside.

It was my dad. He was unloading office supplies and stuff from a big cardboard box.

"Dad, what are you doing?"

"Setting up our home office."

"In the Lincoln Bedroom?"

"It's the only bedroom that isn't being used."

Before I won the election, Dad was a salesman. He sold corrugated cardboard boxes for a company in Wisconsin. My mom was in sales, too. She sold carpet tiles. They both really loved their work, and they weren't sure they were going to move to Washington, because it meant they would have to give up their jobs. In the end, they decided it was more important to be with me.

"Your mother and I decided to start our own business," Dad informed me. "See?" He held up a piece of stationery that read, WHITE HOUSE BOX AND CARPET TILE COMPANY.

"You're going to sell cardboard boxes from the White House?" I asked, incredulous.

"And carpet tiles," he added. "Plenty of people start businesses in their homes nowadays."

"But they don't live in the White House, Dad! It's not cool."

"Are you ashamed of what your mother and I do for a living?" Dad asked, a little hurt.

"No."

"Did you expect us to give up our careers when you became President?"

"No." I hadn't really thought about what my parents were going to do, I had to admit.

"Judson, do you understand how capitalism works? Do you know what free enterprise means?"

"Uh, selling stuff?"

"It's more than that, Jud. It means we live in a country where people compete freely to provide things they think other people want. That's the basis of our American way of life. It's why our standard of living is so high. The government didn't *tell* me to sell cardboard boxes or some other guy to open a restaurant. I discovered there's a need for cardboard boxes, so I'm filling that need. I sell boxes, and I'm proud of it. Starting this business out of the White House is my way of being a good American."

Dad always finds a way to make it seem that life itself revolves around cardboard boxes. He once spent an hour explaining to me what the world would be like if we didn't have cardboard boxes. I won't bore you with the details, but basically civilization collapses because we don't have anything to put stuff in.

"I see what you mean," I sighed. "But if Abraham Lincoln's ghost shows up one night and tells you to get your stuff out of his room, can you move your home office someplace else?"

"Sure, son," he chuckled.

8.
Getting Down
★ to Business ★

"Okay, Mr. President, let's get cracking!" Chief of Staff Lane Brainard said cheerfully when he walked into the Oval Office the first thing Monday morning.

The weekend had been great, but I was excited and anxious to get to work doing good things for America.

"Lane," I began, "when I was campaigning, I promised the children of America the first thing I would do as President would be to abolish homework. So we should start working on that right away."

Lane looked at me with a blank expression on his face.

"You're joking, right, Moon?"

"No, I'm totally serious."

"You don't honestly think the President has the power to abolish homework, do you?"

"Well, yeah," I admitted.

Lane threw back his head and laughed. "You think the President just dreams up new laws and suddenly everybody has to obey them?"

"That's not how it works?"

"Moon, with all due respect, get a clue! This is how it works. Our government is sort of like a tree. There are three big branches. The first is the Executive branch. That's you, the President. The second is the Legislative branch. That's the Senate and House of Representatives, which make up Congress. The third is the Judicial branch. That's the Supreme Court. You follow me so far, Mr. President?"

"Yeah," I said. "But you don't have to call me Mr. President."

"It shows respect for the office, Moon."

"All right, all right," I groaned. "How do you know so much about the government anyway?"

"It's all in the Constitution, Moon. You see, the Founding Fathers of the United States had a revolution against the King of England. So they made sure that our President couldn't get too high and mighty. They worked it out from the start so that the President is no more powerful than Congress. There are strict limits to what you can do."

"What if I want to sign a peace treaty with some other country?" I asked.

"You've got to get the approval of Congress first," Lane explained.

"What if I want to appoint a Supreme Court justice?"

"You've got to get the approval of Congress."

"Well, what if I want to declare war on some foreign country?"

"You've got to get approval," Lane said. "Only Congress has the power to declare war."

"That's not fair," I complained.

"It's perfectly fair," Lane said. "Because it works both ways, Moon. If Congress wants to pass a law that *you* don't like, you can veto it. The Congress has to get the President's approval to do stuff, too. See, it's a system of checks and balances. That way, no one branch can force its will on the others. If one of the three branches is weak, the whole tree falls down. Get it?"

"Wait a minute," I declared. "If the President

can't pass any law he wants, why did you talk me into promising kids I'd make homework illegal?"

"To get votes!" Lane shouted. "So you would win the election!"

"But it forces me to break my promise," I complained. "I don't want to be the kind of President who breaks promises."

"Moon," Lane said, throwing an arm around my shoulders, "don't think of that homework promise as a promise. Think of it as . . . an idea. A bad idea. It would never be passed by Congress, so we'll come up with some other ideas that will."

"I feel bad about letting the kids of America down," I said.

"Forget about them," Lane said. "Kids can't vote anyway."

"Then why did you have me make promises to them?!" I was shouting now.

Lane was about to answer when Honeywell came into the Oval Office. He handed me a copy of *The Washington Post*.

"I thought you might want to see this, sir," he said politely. Then he said he had to go assist Vice-President Syers.

"Oh no!" shouted Lane.

The front page headline read:

SECRET SERVICE MAN
NEARLY DROWNS
AT WHITE HOUSE POOL PARTY

"How could they have found out about that?" I wondered out loud. "There were no reporters there."

"The press has a way of finding out *everything*," Lane sputtered. "One of the kids probably leaked the story." He slammed his fist on the desktop.

"What's the big deal?" I asked. "It's kind of funny."

"Moon," Lane began, lecturing me, "people watch every move you make. You're in a fishbowl now. Everything you do is important. Everybody is going to judge you, criticize you, tape you, photograph you, read your e-mail. I didn't even want them to know you *throw* pool parties. It doesn't look presidential."

"I guess I can't pick my nose in public anymore," I quipped. Lane ignored the remark.

"We'd better start working on your image," he said.

"But I already *won* the election," I protested. "Why do I have to work on my image? Why can't we just do good things for the country? If I do good things for America, won't *that* improve my image?"

Lane snorted. It was the snort he always snorts when I say anything he thinks is horribly naive.

"I've got some ideas that will improve your image," Lane said, pulling out a notebook. "Do you play golf?"

"Never."

"How about jogging?"

"I hate jogging."

"Well, I want you to take up golf and jogging."

"Why?" I asked.

"Because *all* Presidents golf and jog," he explained. "If you want to look presidential, you've got to lose those Rollerblades and get a set of golf clubs. Also, we need to give you a unifying vision."

"A unifying vision? What's that?"

"It's a meaningless expression that sums up

your presidency in three words or less. Kennedy had 'Camelot' and 'New Frontier.' Johnson had 'The Great Society.' Reagan had 'Morning in America.' You need something like that. What do you think of 'New Millennium'?"

"I hate it," I replied.

"It will grow on you," Lane said, checking off something in his notebook. "Next, we need to figure out a way to make an emotional connection to show the public you care about people, without actually having you go out in public."

"Why can't I just go out in public and show I care about people?"

"Because people might try to kill you," he explained. "Now, in Franklin Roosevelt's day, he used to go on the radio every week and talk directly to America. It was called a Fireside Chat. It helped pull the country through the Depression. I think we should revive this idea."

"You want me to go on the radio?"

"No, this is the Information Age," he said. "I have a better idea — the Fireside *Internet* Chat. Once a week, we're going to have you go online and give ordinary citizens the chance to type questions to you. You know, have sort of an interactive conversation with America."

"That's a great idea," I said. "I'll be able to hear their problems, their concerns. I'll be able to keep my finger on the pulse of America."

"Forget about that stuff," Lane scoffed. "The important thing is that it will make you look like you care about the people."

"I *do* care about the people!" I insisted.

"Well, it's more important to *look* like you care than it is to actually care," Lane explained.

"I'll do both," I said.

Lane said he was planning the first Fireside Internet Chat for that evening, so he had to go set things up. As he was leaving the Oval Office, Chief Usher Honeywell escorted Chelsea Daniels in.

I hadn't seen the First Lady since Inauguration Day. Chelsea had been spending most of her time shopping. She looked fabulous, as always. The Secret Service agents in the hall were trying to look at her without being too obvious.

"How's it going, Moon?" Chelsea asked as she

breezed in. She plopped herself down in my chair and put her feet up on my desk.

"Call him Mr. President," Lane corrected her as he walked out. "It's a sign of respect."

Chelsea rolled her eyes and stuck out her tongue. She hadn't been very friendly to Lane ever since he told her he wasn't going to help her become Miss America.

"To what do we owe the pleasure of your company, Miss Daniels?" asked Honeywell.

"I was just dropping off some bills for Moon to sign," she said as she tossed the receipts on my desk.

"I have to get approval from Congress before I sign any bills," I joked as I examined the papers. "Ten thousand dollars . . . for *one* dress?!"

"It's an Oscar de la Renta dress," Chelsea claimed.

"Then why don't you give it back to him?" I suggested. "You know, Chelsea, there are people in this country who are homeless, who are starving."

Chelsea looked at me blankly. She comes from a very wealthy family, and I don't think she's ever met a poor person in her life.

"Moon, you're thirteen years old and you make four hundred thousand dollars a year," she said. "What are you complaining about?"

"I wasn't planning to spend all four hundred thousand on your wardrobe!" I shouted.

"We had a deal, Moon. I would be your First Lady and you would give me an unlimited budget for clothes. Remember?"

"Yes," I admitted reluctantly.

"You're not the kind of President who breaks his promises, are you?"

I thought about my campaign promise to abolish homework. Reluctantly, I handed the bills to Honeywell.

"Pay 'em," I said. Satisfied, Chelsea got up to leave.

"Where are you going now?" I asked.

"Shopping," she replied.

After Lane and Chelsea left, I had a general crummy feeling all over. I usually felt crummy after spending any amount of time with Lane or Chelsea, it occurred to me.

At noon, Honeywell wheeled Vice-President Syers in for our afternoon meeting. She could push her own wheelchair, but Mr. Honeywell seemed to enjoy fussing over her.

"You look like a tomcat who's used up eight of his lives," Vice-President Syers said to me. "What's troublin' my favorite leader of the free world?"

"I don't know," I complained. "I guess I thought being President would be different."

I told Mrs. Syers about my conversation with Lane. I admitted to her that I never realized the President has to get the approval of Congress before he can do just about anything. I had been thinking I was the most powerful person in the world, when actually the President of the United States is pretty weak.

Mrs. Syers rolled her wheelchair up to my desk.

"You ain't no king," she said, taking my hand. "You're a President. You can't do any old thing you wanna do."

"What can the President do, anyway?" I asked.

"One day when I was younger," she said, closing her eyes to remember more clearly, "President Roosevelt came on the radio and told us about

Pearl Harbor being bombed. I remember it like it was yesterday. He said we were going to war. And just by the way he spoke, he made me understand why it was so important that we fight that war. And he made me believe we were going to win in the end. And everybody pitched in to help — men, women, and children. And we *did* win in the end. *That's* what the President can do."

"So the President is sort of the nation's cheerleader?"

"Cheerleader and quarterback," Mrs. Syers replied. "Did Lane tell you about Executive Power?"

"No, what's that?"

"It's special power the President has in a time of emergency. In 1803, Thomas Jefferson used his Executive Power to buy the Louisiana Territory from France. It doubled the size of the country. Jefferson saw the chance, and he took it. He didn't get permission from Congress. He used his Executive Power. And Abraham Lincoln didn't get anybody's approval to free the slaves. He felt it was right. The nation was ripped apart by war. So he used his Executive Power, and it had the force of a law."

"So it's sort of like an extra fire button on a video game."

"You might say that," Mrs. Syers replied.

"But we're not at war now," I pointed out.

"Thank goodness," Mrs. Syers said. "There's no emergency, so you don't need to use your Executive Power. But you have the power to *inspire* us. You nudge the country in the direction you think it oughta go. You can't force it. But you can nudge it. That's how you do good in the world.

"At any moment," she continued, "something terrible could happen. God forbid it ever does. But if it does, you, only you, have the ultimate power to launch a nuclear attack. Just by pressing some buttons in that briefcase. That's your Executive Power. *You* got the power to determine the fate of the world. Still feel weak?"

"I'm glad we talked," I said. "I want to do some good in the world, like we talked about after the election."

"Then you got to stand up for what's right."

"What's right?" I asked.

"That's for you to decide," she explained.

9.
★ Fireside Chat ★

That night, I had my first Fireside Internet Chat with America. Lane came over to the White House so he could sit next to me as I typed my answers to people's questions into the computer. We figured people would be asking some tough questions about the economy and foreign policy, so Lane would be able to help me with the answers.

Ladies and gentlemen,

it said on computer screens all across America at exactly eight o'clock,

Welcome to the first Fireside
Internet Chat with the President of the
United States.

In the corner of the screen was a little fireplace with a simulated fire burning. A computer-generated version of "Hail to the Chief" came out of the speaker, one of Lane's clever little touches.

Hello, America, I typed.
I welcome your questions and comments.

We waited a few seconds and then the responses came scrolling up the screen faster than I could read them:

SUZYQ: Moon is the greatest President since Lincoln!
HOT ROD: You're an IDIOT! Moon is way better than Lincoln.
BLUEBOY: I disagree with that.
SSSNAKE: Who asked U, moron?
JELLYROLL: Hey, SuzyQ, what U look like?

"This isn't working out quite the way I planned," Lane said. "Ask them if they have any questions."

This is President Moon, I typed.
Does anyone have any QUESTIONS?
BADBOY: Yeah, do U wear boxers or briefs?
OOBYDOOBY: Anybody got a laser printer
they wanna sell?
CHAMELEON: Just ignore these jerks, Mr.
President.
MOLINA: Moon rocks.
MISS MOLLY: I LOVE MOON!!!!!!
GOLLYWOG: How do I log outta here?
RATTLESNAKE: Mr. President, will U marry
me?
CCR: Moon is my hero.
LODI: Moon = the man.
JFOG: Mr. President, I want to apologize on
behalf of all Americans. These people are
stupid.
MARY: Hey, who ya calling stupid? You're
the stupid one!
HERICANE: Is this the web site of the
Wilma Flintstone Fan Club?
BAYOU: How do I get a date with the First
Lady? She's HOT!

After an hour, we logged off. The people of
America *did* seem to approve of me. But Lane
and I decided to abandon the Fireside Internet
Chat for the time being.

10.
★ The Endless Parade ★

Once I understood how the White House and the presidency basically worked, I was ready to put the wheels of government into motion. I encouraged Chief of Staff Lane Brainard to prepare a full schedule for me. The more appointments I had during the day, I figured, the more I would be able to accomplish, the more good I could do for the country.

Lane told me exactly how to handle my appointments. When somebody entered the Oval Office, he explained, I should shake hands, greet him or her, chat for a few minutes, and pose for a photo. Then I should look at my watch and apologize that I couldn't spend more time with the person. Lane would escort the guest out and whisk in the next appointment.

"Bring 'em on," I said.

My first appointment was with a group of newspaper editors. I shook hands, made a little small talk, posed for photos, and told them I was sorry I couldn't spend more time with them. They seemed thrilled to be in the White House and didn't complain when twenty minutes were up.

I barely had the chance to catch my breath when Lane brought in a senior citizens' group. After twenty minutes they were gone, replaced by a women's group.

A group of disabled veterans was next, followed by some Elvis impersonators, who sang a song. Then came a garden club. Some animal lovers. An organization that wanted to abolish Daylight Saving Time.

One after another they came and went. I presented some people with plaques that Lane had made up. People gave me gifts. I met with a team of kids who almost won the Little League World Series. A writer from *Boy's Life* interviewed me. I was introduced to some people who contributed money to my campaign just so they could get their picture taken with me and put it on their walls at home.

After a while, I gave up trying to pay attention to who they were and why they were there. I just shook hands, said hello, posed for pictures, and they were gone.

Mayors came and went. Senators. Governors. There might have been a few kings in there, though I'm not sure, because after a while they all blended in with one another. It didn't matter how important they were. Lane shuffled them in and out of the Oval Office like they were customers at Taco Bell.

It was mind-numbing. After a few hours of meeting and greeting, my head was spinning. The barrage of flashbulbs was giving me after-images — black spots floating before my eyes.

"Keep smiling," Lane said between appointments. "You're doing great."

The parade through the Oval Office continued. I met with some college kids who built a car that runs on solar power. A barbershop quartet sang "Sweet Adeline" to me. Then I met the ambassador from a foreign country I'd never heard of. He was followed by the Michigan Apple Queen. Or maybe she was the Wisconsin Cheese Queen. Whoever she was, she was wearing a crown and left something edible that made a stain on my desk.

One after another, the endless parade continued, and everybody had a picture taken with me.

"We're going to get great press coverage tomorrow," Lane said gleefully. "Wait until you see the headlines. You're doing a terrific job. These people love you. Keep smiling."

After a few more appointments, it was getting late in the afternoon. I was totally exhausted. It was a relief when Lane said there was only one more appointment left on the day's schedule.

"Who is it?" I asked wearily.

"An organization that calls itself CMLMIMD, sir."

"What does that stand for?"

"I don't know."

"Send 'em in," I said, suppressing a yawn. Lane brought two men and a woman into the Oval Office.

"It's a pleasure to meet you, President Moon," the woman said as she curtsied and shook my hand.

"The pleasure is all mine," I replied. Lane had

told me that anytime someone said what a pleasure it was to meet me, I should always reply that the pleasure was all mine.

"President Moon," one of the men said, clearing his throat nervously, "we realize you're busy so we won't waste your time with small talk."

"I appreciate that," I said. "It's been a long day."

"For about one hundred years," the man continued, "people have been calling breakfast the most important meal of the day. We believe that, in fact, *lunch* is far more important than breakfast. And we believe it is a gross injustice to perpetrate this hoax on the American people."

"Excuse me," I interrupted. "What's the name of your organization?"

"The CMLMIMD, sir," the other man chimed in. "The Committee to Make Lunch the Most Important Meal of the Day."

"Would you excuse me for one moment?" I asked, and pulled Lane aside to talk in private.

"Are these people nuts?" I whispered.

"I'm not sure," he whispered back.

"Who cares which is the most important meal of the day?"

"Moon, they apparently care a lot."

"Why am I wasting my time with these bozos?"

"They contributed five million dollars to your campaign, Moon."

"So what?"

"It could be argued that you wouldn't have been elected President without their help."

I went back to the smiling CMLMIMD people. "I'm sorry," I said. "Please continue."

"It is our belief," the lady said, "that lunch has been a second-class citizen for too long. Lots of people skip breakfast or just wolf down a Pop Tart. We feel the time is long overdue to right this wrong and give lunch the credit it de--serves."

"We'd like to discuss it with you tomorrow," the first guy said. "Perhaps over lunch?"

"That's it!" I shouted. "Get out of here!"

"What?" the three of them said, shocked.

"Mr. President!" Lane yelled, trying to stop me from saying anything else. Secret Service Agent Doe peeked in the door to see what was going on.

"Get these people out of here!" I hollered.

"You and your organization are a bunch of losers who have too much time on your hands!"

"So this is how you treat your contributors," the lady said angrily, pointing her finger at me. "Well, we got you elected, Moon, and we can ruin you, too!"

"Get a life, lady!" I shouted as Agent Doe grabbed her.

"Hey, we never got our picture taken with the President!" one of the men complained as the guards dragged him away.

"Beat it!" I screamed.

"Moon! You can't kick your supporters out of the Oval Office!" Lane complained after the whole fuss was over.

"They're morons," I said. "Where did idiots like that get five million dollars anyway?"

"By skipping a lot of breakfasts and dinners, I guess," Lane said. "But Moon, you've got to understand how politics works. When somebody does a politician a favor, they expect a favor in return. Would it really hurt anybody if you named lunch the most important meal of the day?"

"I guess not," I said wearily.

At the end of the day, I could barely keep my eyes open. I hadn't set foot outside all day. I hadn't seen my parents. I thought about taking a swim in the White House pool or playing some video games in the game room. But I was so tired, I just collapsed on my bed and was asleep in minutes.

When I woke up the next morning, I opened *The Washington Post* to see this big headline:

MOON THROWS TANTRUM!
VISITORS CLAIM PREZ WENT
BERSERK IN OVAL OFFICE!

And this smaller one:

Lunch Named
Most Important
Meal of the Day

11.
The Secret Ninja
★ Death Touch ★

Having a Secret Service agent watch your every move is creepy.

Everywhere I turned, Agent Doe was there. When I woke up in the morning, he was outside my bedroom door, waiting for me. When I went to sleep at night, he was there. He never seemed to sleep or eat. He was always hanging around, twenty feet away from me, watching me but pretending not to.

The weird thing is, after a while, I got used to it. I stopped noticing him lurking in the shadows. He became like a piece of furniture. A piece of furniture that carried a gun and just happened to move wherever I moved, like one magnet being pulled along by another magnet.

Chief of Staff Lane Brainard told me to take up jogging, but the President can't just go outside alone. Agent Doe had to go with me. I thought he was going to complain, but he didn't. At more than 300 pounds, he knew he could use the exercise.

We jogged early in the morning, before the streets were filled with people. Leaving from the White House, we could usually make it to the Lincoln Memorial and back in less than an hour. We must have been a sight, this enormous bald-headed black man jogging with a skinny thirteen-year-old white boy. Trailing behind us was always a car with Secret Service agents inside holding the football.

Each morning, Agent Doe led me on a different route. He said that if we went the same way every day, it would be easier for somebody to try to harm me. It seemed ridiculous, but when it came to security, Agent Doe was my boss.

As we jogged, little by little he told me about himself. He was from California. He'd never met his father, he said. His mom couldn't afford to send him to college, so he put himself through school by working as a bouncer in a bar. A bouncer is a big guy who breaks up fights and kicks out people who get rowdy.

He didn't like that job, so he joined the Army. He fought in the Gulf War, and his bravery was noticed by one of the generals. Soon Doe was with the Secret Service, assigned to protect President Bush.

I guess they figured he was so big that if some nut ever tried to shoot the President, Agent Doe would make the perfect human shield. Still, he said he'd always had a weight problem. Several times he had received warnings about it from the head of the Secret Service.

He didn't have any brothers or sisters, and he never got married. When I asked him why not, he said he was "married to his job."

From the start, I had been bugging Agent Doe about teaching me some martial arts. I had taken a few tae kwon do classes when I was younger and learned a few moves, but he was an expert.

"Did you ever hurt anybody really badly?" I asked as we jogged past the Washington Monument early one morning.

"Yes," he puffed. "But only in self-defense, Mr. President."

"What happened?"

"It was in the bar, sir," he said. "Some guy got

drunk and was bothering people. I asked him politely to leave. He wouldn't. So I asked him again, a little less politely. He smashed a bottle against the bar and came at me with it. I had to subdue him."

"What did you do?"

"Oh, I know a few tricks, sir."

"Will you teach them to me?" I asked.

"I don't know about that, sir," he huffed. "They're very dangerous."

"Please?" I begged.

"As long as I'm around, sir, you don't need to bother yourself with that stuff."

I kept after Agent Doe, begging and pleading him to show me his martial arts techniques. I threatened to have him thrown into the White House pool again. I just about used my Executive Power to force him to spill the beans.

I wore him down, I guess. Finally, he agreed to teach me the secret of how to disable a man in three seconds.

After a morning jog, we went up to the roof of the White House, where there was plenty of room for hand-to-hand combat and nobody around to disturb us.

"Can I hit you really hard?" I asked before we got started.

"Go ahead, sir," Agent Doe said. "But you don't have to use all your strength to immobilize a man."

I took a little running start and gave him my best shot, a reverse knife hand strike right below the chest. I wasn't expecting to knock him down or anything, but I thought I might be able to rock him back a little.

Nothing doing. It was like hitting a refrigerator.

"Owww!" I yelled, shaking my hand.

"Mr. President, are you okay?" Agent Doe rushed to comfort me.

"I'll be fine," I grimaced.

"If you get hurt, I'm in big trouble, sir."

"Don't worry about it," I assured him.

"You're just a little guy, sir, so you shouldn't go running and charging at big guys like me," he explained. "Let me show you something that might work better — the Secret Ninja Death Touch."

"Yeah!" I agreed excitedly, "the Secret Ninja Death Touch. That sounds cool. How do I do it?"

"The Secret Ninja Death Touch is a part of dim-mak. Death-point striking, it's called," Agent Doe explained. "It's the deadliest system of self-defense ever created. You should only use it in life-or-death situations. There are only a few dim-mak masters in the world."

"Where did you learn it?"

"From a guy I met in the Gulf War. He learned it from a sergeant who fought in Vietnam. And *he* learned it from a South Vietnamese dim-mak master."

"What do I do?"

"The idea is that you can totally immobilize an opponent by applying intense pressure to his most vulnerable areas. There are forty-three major target areas on the human body. They are neurological shutdown points. If you interrupt and manipulate your attacker's nervous and circulatory systems, those systems shut down almost instantly."

"Awesome!"

"In the first second he feels pain," Agent Doe explained. "In the second, numbness sets in. And in the third, he becomes unconscious."

"What happens in the fourth second?" I asked.

"Death," he said simply. "That's why it's called the Secret Ninja Death Touch."

"And you don't even have to hit the guy?"

"Correct, sir. Go ahead, grab me from behind."

I went behind Agent Doe's back and wrapped my arm around his huge neck.

"Okay, you got me good and tight, right, sir?" he asked.

"Right."

"I can't escape, right?"

"Right."

At that point, Agent Doe reached behind him and placed his thumb on a part of my body. I can't tell you what part because I know that if I did, some of you lunatics reading this would go and try it on your friends. You're going to have to take my word for this. He touched me with his thumb and put pressure on that part of my body.

I didn't feel anything at first, but after about a second I felt a little numb.

"See? You're helpless, aren't you?"

"Yeah," I grunted.

"If I wanted to totally immobilize you I would increase the pressure," Agent Doe explained. "In a few seconds you would pass out. But I won't do that, of course, because . . ."

That was the last thing I remember before I passed out.

12.
★ A Deadly Mistake ★

"President Moon! Mr. President!" shouted Chief Usher Honeywell. He and the White House doctor were leaning over me, holding a cold washcloth against my forehead. All I knew was that I was alive, and I was lying down somewhere.

"Wh-what happened?" I asked foggily. "Where am I?"

"On the roof of the White House, sir," Honeywell explained. "You were unconscious!"

"I'm sorry, Mr. President," blubbered Secret Service Agent Doe. "It was an accident!"

I looked up and saw that three other Secret Service agents were holding Agent Doe's arms behind his back, the way cops on TV hold criminals. They were snapping handcuffs around

Agent Doe's wrists. His gun had been taken away from him.

"You have the right to remain silent," one of the agents explained to Agent Doe. "Anything you say may be used against you —"

"I wasn't trying to hurt the President!" sobbed Agent Doe. "You've got to believe me! Protecting the President is my whole life! It's the only thing I care about!"

The agents started dragging Agent Doe away.

"Wait!" I said, struggling to my feet. "Take the handcuffs off him. He's telling the truth."

The agents stopped dragging Agent Doe away, but they didn't let go of him.

"It was all my fault," I explained. "I forced him to show me some martial arts moves. I didn't tell him to stop in time. Let him go, please."

In five minutes, the head of the Secret Service arrived at the White House. He wanted to fire Agent Doe immediately. Even though I was okay, he said that if word got out about the incident, it would make the Secret Service look bad.

I insisted that Agent Doe not be fired. He received a harsh reprimand but was allowed to continue in his job. Everyone who witnessed the incident agreed not to tell any reporters about it.

"I'm sorry, Mr. President," Agent Doe said when it was all over and everyone had gone back to their posts. "It will never happen again, sir."

"That's right," I said with a smile. "I know the Secret Ninja Death Touch now. Next time I'm going to kick your butt."

He didn't laugh, but I thought I might have caught him half smiling.

Front page of The Washington Post, *March 19:*

SECRET SERVICE AGENT ALMOST KILLS PRESIDENT!

THE PEOPLE SPEAK

★★★★★

"Do you approve or disapprove of the way President Moon is doing his job?"

74% Approve

20% Disapprove

6% Undecided

13.

★ **Miller the Killer** ★

Shortly after I was sworn in as President, Chief Usher Honeywell came into the Oval Office and announced, "Mr. President, your tutor is here."

"T-tutor?" I stammered.

"Sir, it's not like I just told you World War III has begun. It's just the White House tutor."

"Nobody told me I would have a tutor," I protested.

"Did you think becoming President meant you would get to miss four years of school, sir?"

"No, I just . . . figured I . . . would be learning a lot on the job."

"All children must attend school, sir. Even if the child happens to be President of the United States. A regular school would pose security risks to you. That's why we have a tutor. Don't worry. Mrs. Miller is excellent. She taught President Clinton's daughter. She taught President Ford's children. She has taught all the children who lived in the White House for as far back as I can remember."

"Oh, all right," I agreed reluctantly, "send her in."

Honeywell left and a little old lady walked into the Oval Office alone. She was wearing one of those weird black mesh hats that is sort of like a doily that sits on top of your head. I think they issue them to women on their ninetieth birthday. That's about how old Mrs. Miller had to be. She seemed too weak and fragile to still be teaching at her age.

"So you're the kid who became President, eh?" Mrs. Miller sneered, looking me over carefully. "You must think you're pretty smart."

"Well, no, I really —"

"Quiet!" she scolded me. "That wasn't a question. Don't you have the manners to raise your hand in class?"

Class? I looked around, just checking to make sure there weren't any other kids.

"Tell me, Mr. Smarty-Pants," Mrs. Miller continued, "what was the name of the Pilgrims' ship?"

"Uh . . . the *Mayflower*?" I guessed.

"Hmm, you got lucky on that one," she smirked, pacing the floor like a tiger circling its prey. "Who was our third President?"

"Uh . . . John Adams?"

"No!" Mrs. Miller shrieked. "Thomas Jefferson! When I was a child, I could name all the Presidents, backward and forward."

I thought about saying there had probably only been three or four Presidents when she was a child, but I kept my mouth shut.

"Now tell me, young man. What's thirteen times thirteen?"

"Uh . . . I need a calculator," I said with a shrug.

"Use the one in your *head*!" she yelled. She had her face right up close to mine now. I felt myself starting to sweat. "How do you spell *coincidence*?"

"C-O-I-N-S —"

"Wrong!" she screamed into my ear. "You

must know *this* — who was the first person to set foot on the moon?"

"Uh . . . Armstrong?"

"What is his *first* name?"

His first name. His first name. I knew it. I knew I knew it. It was on the tip of my tongue.

"Louis," I finally said.

"*Neil* Armstrong!" she shrieked. "Louis Armstrong was a trumpet player. How do you expect to run this country if you think a trumpet player walked on the moon?"

I raised my hand timidly.

"What do you want?" Mrs. Miller barked.

"May I be excused?" I asked. "I need to use the bathroom."

"You should have thought of that before," she said disgustedly. "Get in your seat. Today you're going to learn the history of the United States. If you want to be a good President, you have to know your history."

I slunk back around my desk and sat down. I wasn't feeling very presidential.

For the next hour and a half, Mrs. Miller taught me the history of the United States. From the *beginning*. She told me how the earth used to be a big molten rock spinning through space. Over millions of years, it gradually cooled and the continents formed. They all floated around until North America ended up where it was.

I was tempted to ask her if she knew all this stuff from memory, but I didn't dare. I snuck a peek at my watch. She had been talking for an hour, and she was only up to the Ice Age. By the time she got to World War I, I figured, I'd be *her* age. My bladder felt like it was about to explode.

Finally, Mrs. Miller finished the lesson. She stopped at the point where human beings had arrived in North America, but they hadn't learned how to use tools yet. Mrs. Miller said tomorrow she would pick up where we left off. She gave me a huge pile of homework. Then she marched out of the Oval Office.

Not a second too soon! I ran to the bathroom just before the dam burst. When I got back to the Oval Office, Chief of Staff Lane Brainard was waiting for me.

"So, how did it go with Mrs. Miller?" Lane asked.

"Miller the Killer," I moaned. I told Lane what Mrs. Miller had taught me and he just laughed.

"The President doesn't need to know any of that prehistoric junk," he snorted. "That's why it's called *pre*historic. It's before history began. I can tell you everything you need to know about American history in ten minutes."

"On your mark . . . get set . . . go," I said, looking at my watch.

"Okay, Christopher Columbus discovered America in 1492," Lane began, "but Indians were already here so he really didn't discover anything. And besides, Columbus only went to the Bahamas on his first trip over."

"My folks went there on vacation once," I added.

"Great, Moon," Lane said, unimpressed. "So tell me what happened after Columbus arrived?"

"Uh, he returned to England?"

"*Spain*, Moon. You really *don't* know anything, do you? The next important thing that happened was that the Pilgrims came to America in search of religious freedom in 1620. You know, the *Mayflower*, Plymouth Rock, Thanksgiving, all that stuff."

"Wait a minute," I interrupted. "Didn't anything important happen during the hundred years or so between Columbus and the Pilgrims?"

"Nothing that you need to concern yourself with, Moon."

"Okay," I said. "So what happened next?"

"The British established the thirteen colonies."

"Thirteen is bad luck."

"It was for *them*," Lane agreed. "They taxed the colonies heavily, so the colonists revolted in 1775. Paul Revere rode. Patrick Henry said, 'Give me liberty or give me death!' Thomas Jefferson wrote the Declaration of Independence. And George Washington led the colonies to victory in the Revolutionary War."

"And he was elected the first President," I said.

"Right. And the Founding Fathers wrote the Constitution in 1787. Everything was cool going into the 1800s."

"Wow," I marveled. "You just covered two hundred years in five minutes."

"But in the next two hundred years a lot more

stuff happened," Lane informed me. "The United States grew and spread across North America from the Atlantic to the Pacific."

"That was good, right?"

"Well, to do it we had to fight another war with England, go to war with Mexico, and just about wipe out the Indians."

"And that was bad, right?" I asked.

"Right. But then Abraham Lincoln was elected our sixteenth President in 1860."

"That was good, right?" I asked.

"Yeah, but the Southern states left the Union to form their own country, the Confederacy."

"Why'd they do that?" I asked.

"Mostly because they wanted slavery to continue and Lincoln wanted to abolish it. The North and South fought the Civil War. Six hundred thousand Americans were killed . . . by other Americans."

"Very bad."

"Yeah," Lane said, "but in the end the nation was preserved and slavery was abolished."

"That was good."

"Yeah, but five days after the war was over, Lincoln was assassinated."

"Very bad."

"Yeah, but after the Civil War the United States slowly recovered. Great new machines like the telegraph, telephone, automobile, lightbulb, and airplane made the United States strong and prosperous."

"And that was good."

"Yeah, but then we got drawn into World War I."

"Bad, right?" I asked.

"Yeah, but our side won, so it turned out okay. The Roaring Twenties came. The nation was prosperous. Women got the vote. Everybody was happy."

"That's good."

"It was, until the stock market crashed in 1929 and the Great Depression started."

"Bad?" I asked.

"Awful," Lane said. "Millions of people were out of work. Banks failed. People starved. Tough times. But then Franklin D. Roosevelt was elected President and he led us out of the Depression."

"Which was good."

"Yeah, until Hitler came to power in Germany and started World War II."

"Bad."

"Yeah, but we won the war."

"Good?"

"Yeah, but we developed the atomic bomb to win the war."

"Bad?" I asked. "Or good?"

"Both. The bomb ended World War II, which was good. But it killed hundreds of thousands of innocent people. And it prompted the Soviet Union and other countries to start building nuclear weapons, too."

"Bad."

"Yeah," Lane said. "The Cold War began, which led to wars in Korea and Vietnam."

"Bad."

"Yeah, but eventually the Soviet Union broke up and the Cold War was over."

Lane got up, like he was finished and ready to go.

"And then?" I asked.

"And then, Moon, you got elected President."

I sat back in my chair and looked at my watch.

It had been ten minutes, almost to the second. Four hundred years of American history summed up in ten minutes.

"So that's it?" I asked.

"Pretty much," Lane said. "I left a lot of stuff out, but you've got the basics."

"So what happens next, Lane?"

"Who knows, Moon?" Lane said. "Maybe that's up to *you*."

14.
Some Enchanted
★ Evening! ★

"Judson, clean your room!" Mom shouted one morning in June.

"Aw, Mom!" I complained, "I gotta get ready for tomorrow's meetings and the big dinner party tonight."

"Just because you're President doesn't mean you don't have to pick up after yourself."

"Aw, give me a break, Mom."

"And get dressed. Judson, you know I don't like it when you brush your teeth in your underwear."

"Mom, I don't even *have* teeth in my underwear."

"Don't be smart with me, young man. I can still put you in time out."

"Mom, I could put you in *jail*."

All in all, I was getting along with my parents

pretty well. They seemed to be dealing with the fact that I was more powerful than they were. The White House Box and Carpet Tile Company turned out to be a good move after all. It gave them something to do, so they couldn't spend too much time telling *me* what to do.

A big part of the President's job, I discovered, is to host parties. There's a dinner party at the White House just about every week.

Now, *my* idea of a good party is to order a pizza and invite some friends over to play video games. But when people like the Queen of England and the President of Venezuela are coming over, they expect something a little fancier. Fortunately, that was an area in which First Lady Chelsea Daniels was an expert.

When it was time for my first state dinner in the White House, I put Chelsea in charge of everything — invitations, seating arrangements, menu, music, everything. When she was finished, the State Dining Room looked spectacular.

"This will be the greatest party of my life,"

Chelsea said excitedly as the State Dining Room was being readied for the big night.

"There will be important people from all over the world here tonight," Honeywell said as he helped me put on my tuxedo. "So be careful not to do anything that might offend anyone."

"What do you think I'm gonna do," I asked, "wipe my nose on the King of Spain?"

"Some foreign countries have unusual customs," he replied, ignoring my remark. "Don't let King Fahd of Saudi Arabia see you eating with your left hand. In his country they consider that unclean. And snapping your fingers is vulgar to the French. If you give the thumbs-up sign to the Afghani ambassador, he'll think you're cursing him out. Don't mention World War II to the German or Japanese diplomats, and don't bring up apartheid to the South Africans."

"I don't even know what apartheid *means*," I said.

"Good," Honeywell replied, buttoning my shirt. "Make sure you don't yawn in front of Colombian President Pastrana. And whatever you do, don't compliment the Moroccans on their clothing. They'll take them off right there and *give* them to you."

It was too much to take in at once. "Let's just get this over with," I moaned. My tux was about as comfortable as wearing a suit made of barbed wire.

We went up to the beauty salon, on the third floor, to get Chelsea. For a brainless airhead who only cared about the way she looked, I had to admit she looked *terrific*. She was wearing a dark blue strapless dress, embroidered top to bottom in pearls and sequins. Seeing her took my breath away.

"Moon," Chelsea smiled, taking my arm, "in a tuxedo you look . . . almost handsome." I think that was the first time Chelsea Daniels said anything nice to me.

Honeywell gave us the signal, and Chelsea and I walked down the big staircase to greet our guests in the Diplomatic Reception Room.

There were more than a hundred people milling around, all dressed in tuxedos and gowns. Kings and queens. Presidents and their wives. Princes and princesses. Diplomats and ambassadors. The most powerful people on earth. If a bomb were dropped on the White House at that moment, I thought, well, it would level the place and I'd be dead.

Soon, everybody was escorted into the State Dining Room for dinner. I was seated between my mother and Chelsea. Dad was at another table, where I saw him hobnobbing with the Prime Minister of Pakistan and Vice-President Syers.

The chattering of dozens of different languages filled the room. I spotted Secret Service Agent Doe in the corner, keeping a watchful eye on things. Honeywell hung around a few feet behind me. Whenever anyone came over to greet me, Honeywell would quickly whisper the person's name in my ear.

I looked down at the place setting before me. It was frightening. There were three glasses, two plates, a cloth napkin, four forks, three knives, two spoons, and a few scattered utensils I couldn't identify.

"This is a perfect example of government

waste," I pointed out to Chelsea. "We could save the taxpayers millions of dollars by getting rid of some of this useless silverware."

"Relax, Moon," Chelsea whispered. "You start with the fork farthest away from the plate. As each course is taken away, you pick up the next fork. Once you pick up a utensil, it should never touch the table again."

Chelsea didn't know anything about anything, but she seemed to know *everything* when it came to dressing, shopping, and fancy dinner parties.

"Sit up straight, Judson," my mother whispered. "And get your elbows off the table. Everybody's watching you."

"I'm the most powerful man in the world, Mom," I said, putting my napkin on my lap. "I'll put my elbows wherever I want."

"Don't tilt your chair back," Chelsea whispered.

"Stop waving your napkin around like a flag," Mom muttered under her breath. "And stop picking your teeth. You want everyone to think the President of the United States is a pig?"

Everything I did seemed to be wrong, so I decided to just sit there like a statue.

"Show a little life, Moon!" Chelsea whispered. "You're the host."

When everybody was seated, Premier Li Peng of China stood up and raised his glass. Everybody quieted down.

"I'd like to propose a toast to the President of the United States," he said in perfect English. "May he rule in peace and prosperity. *Gan bei.*"

"What's *gan bei*?" I whispered, turning around to Honeywell.

"Bottoms up, sir."

"What's in the glass?" I whispered.

"Grapefruit juice," he whispered back. "You're too young to drink alcohol."

"I'm allergic to grapefruit juice."

"Sir, it would be an insult to Premier Li and his country if you refuse to drink with him."

"But I was taught not to give in to peer pressure."

"Sir," Honeywell said with some urgency, "it could cause an international incident if you refuse."

Everyone in the room was staring at me. I

stood up, raised my glass toward the Chinese Premier, and downed it. Everyone burst into applause. The juice was awful.

When I went to sit back down, Honeywell whispered, "It is customary for you to propose a toast in return, sir."

"Do I have to?" I choked.

"Just sip it," Honeywell suggested.

I stood up again.

"I, too, would like to propose a toast," I announced as a waiter filled my glass. "To my honored guest from China, and all my guests. May we live in healthy, happy, and peaceful times. *Ben gay.*"

"I believe you mean *gan bei*, sir," whispered Honeywell. "Ben-Gay is an ointment for sore muscles."

"*Gan bei*," I announced.

After the toast, the waiters brought around little salads. Everyone sat around awkwardly. I was really hungry, but nobody else was eating yet. I didn't want to look impolite by eating before the others. My stomach was growling and the lettuce was wilting on my plate.

"When do we eat?" I asked Honeywell. "I'm starving."

"It is traditional that guests do not touch their silverware until the President begins to eat, sir."

I looked around the room. Everyone was watching me. I picked up my fork. Everyone picked up their forks. As soon as I dug in, so did everyone else.

I finished the salad in about five seconds and was ready for more food. The waiters swooped in with the next course. Everybody oohed and ahhed over the food, but it looked gross to me. I asked the waiter what it was.

"Beef bouilli with horseradish sauce, Mr. President."

"It's delicious!" Chelsea beamed. "Just taste it, Moon."

I tasted it. It tasted as gross as it looked. I thought I was going to die.

"What else have you got?" I asked.

"Sir, the next course will be squash soup, followed by poached salmon with egg sauce. Then we will be bringing out roast supreme of duckling à l'orange with raisins and crab claws with dill mustard sauce. Finally, dessert will be our pastry chef's specialty, marzipan en surprise."

I started to feel a little nauseous.

"Do you think I could get a Big Mac?" I asked the waiter. "I don't like any of that stuff."

"A Big Mac, sir?"

"It's a burger. Two all-beef patties, special sauce —"

"Moon, you don't ask for fast food at a state dinner!" Chelsea scolded me. "You're humiliating me!"

"Well, I'm not eating *this* stuff," I told her. I asked the waiter to get me some french fries, too. "That ought to make the President of France happy," I pointed out.

The waiter hurried off. While I waited for my burger to arrive, a few people came over to greet me. In each case, Honeywell told me who each person was as he or she approached.

"Mr. President," Honeywell whispered, "the man walking toward you is Supreme Ruler Raul Trujillo, friendly dictator of Cantania, a small nation in South America."

"Ah, Supreme Ruler Trujillo," I said, extending my hand. "It is a pleasure meet you."

He didn't put out his hand, and he didn't say the pleasure was all his. I pretended to brush some invisible lint off my pants with the hand he wouldn't shake. Trujillo looked a little drunk. He just stared at me.

"So," I said, struggling to make conversation, "do dictators do a lot of . . . dictation?"

"I see the United States has sent a boy to do a man's job," Trujillo said gruffly but in surprisingly good English.

"Uh, yes," I replied. "We kids figured grownups had more than two hundred years to mess everything up, and now it's our turn. How did you like your salad?"

"I'm sure you realize, President Moon," Trujillo sneered, "that without your planes and guns and bombs, my country would crush yours like an insect."

"In that case," I replied, "I'm glad we've got all those planes and guns and bombs."

Trujillo didn't laugh at my joke. He grunted and walked away, muttering, "Until we meet again, President Moon."

I grabbed Honeywell. "I thought you said that guy was a *friendly* dictator."

"He is," Honeywell replied. "You should meet the *un*friendly ones."

My burger finally arrived and I wolfed it down in seconds. There were no fries and I was still hungry.

As the waiters finally cleared away the dishes, the Marine Band set up their instruments and began to play. A few couples got up to dance. Chelsea looked around awkwardly.

"Mr. President," Honeywell whispered, "it is customary for the President and First Lady to dance."

"I don't know how to dance," I said. "And I don't feel so well."

"Didn't you ever take dancing lessons, Moon?" Chelsea complained.

"If I ever took dancing lessons," I told her, "the guys at school would have beaten me to a pulp."

"Just fake it," she said, grabbing me by the hand and pulling me up. I handed the football to Agent Doe so I could dance.

I stepped on Chelsea's feet a few times, but I don't think I caused any internal bleeding or anything. We danced over to my mom and dad. They seemed to be having the time of their lives.

"How was dinner, Dad?" I asked.

"Great!" he exclaimed. "I just talked the President of Pakistan into buying fifty thousand cardboard boxes."

"Let's dance over near the bathroom," I told Chelsea.

"Why?"

"I think I might have to barf."

"That's disgusting!" Chelsea said before dashing back to the table.

After dinner, everybody was mixing and mingling. They all wanted to meet me, and I did my best to be polite. But it was hard, because I was tired and hungry. No matter what I did, somebody always seemed to get mad.

The ambassador from Paraguay got upset when I crossed my fingers, which is apparently some kind of obscene gesture in his country. I offended the Prime Minister of Taiwan just because he saw me *blink.* The Grand Duke of Luxembourg got mad when I refused to kiss him on the cheek, and he walked out of the White House in a huff.

The party was starting to break up when a guy with a white apron and one of those big chef hats marched over to me.

"I don't care if you're the President!" he shouted. "You are uncouth! You show me no respect by refusing my food! I quit!"

"Who *are* you?"

"I am the king of marzipan!"

"I don't care what country you come from," I said. "When am I going to get those fries I asked for?"

He tore off his apron, threw it on the floor, and stormed away.

By the end of the evening I had unintentionally insulted people of just about every race and nationality. A few of them looked like they were ready to declare war on the United States.

"You ruined my party!" Chelsea sobbed, running upstairs.

I never did get my french fries, and I was still hungry. When everybody had left, I sneaked downstairs to the White House kitchen to grab a bite to eat. I was poking around the cabinets and couldn't find anything good.

There *must* be something yummy in the refrigerator, I figured. The door to the fridge was enormous, about the size of a garage door. I had to use all my strength to open it.

The light went on and I walked into the fridge. Just about every food you can imagine was in there. I had my choice of cakes and pies, steaks, burgers, chicken, everything. I rubbed my hands together to keep them warm.

And then the door shut behind me and the light went out.

Front page of The Washington Post, *June 23:*

FOREIGN RELATIONS CHILL
AS MOON LOCKS SELF
IN WHITE HOUSE FRIDGE

15.
★ More Disaster Areas ★

I was locked in the White House refrigerator for about an hour — in the dark — until I found an emergency alarm switch. Security guards came running from all over and pulled me out, shaking and shivering. I've had more embarrassing moments in my life, but I couldn't think of any.

After the state dinner disaster, more bad news arrived. First, a horrific hurricane ripped through Florida, tearing the state up. There was billions of dollars' worth of damage. Thousands of people lost their homes. A photo on the front page of *The Washington Post* showed somebody's *house* actually flying through the air. That's how bad the storm was. Lane said I should go to Florida to show the people down there that I was concerned.

Next to the photo of the flying house was an article about First Lady Chelsea Daniels. That was the second bit of bad news.

FIRST LADY HAS WORTHY CAUSE: HERSELF

the headline read. The Philadelphia *Inquirer* also had an article about Chelsea, with the headline:

FIRST LADY PUTS FIRST LADY FIRST

It seems that some investigative reporters had followed Chelsea around for a week to see what she did all day. They found out that she pretty much went from store to store, spending a fortune on designer clothes for herself.

"This looks bad," Lane said. "There are people who lost everything they owned in the hurricane, and here's the First Lady, who only cares about how she looks."

As Lane and I were reading the article, Chelsea happened to flounce into the Oval Office and fling more bills on my desk.

"Ta ta, boys," she said.

"Did you happen to see today's paper?" I asked before Chelsea could leave.

"Why read the papers?" she asked. "They only print bad news."

I showed her the *Washington Post* headline. She glanced at it briefly and slammed it on my desk angrily.

"How *dare* they write such lies about me!" she exclaimed. "Why don't you have these newspapers shut down, Moon? You're the President."

"We have freedom of the press in this country," I informed her. "Newspapers can write whatever they want. Maybe you should read the Bill of Rights."

"I don't read bills," Chelsea said. "I just give them to you to pay."

That got Lane mad. "Not only do you waste the President's money," he shouted at Chelsea, "you make him look bad."

"Don't blame *me* if Moon looks bad!" Chelsea shot right back. "*I* didn't get sick at a dinner party and lock myself in a refrigerator! *I* didn't drown any Secret Service agents! I'm the only thing that makes Moon look *good* around here."

She had a point, I had to admit. Just about

everything I did seemed to backfire, create negative headlines, and hurt my approval rating.

"Chelsea," Lane said more gently, "in the past, First Ladies have devoted themselves to good causes. Barbara Bush worked for literacy. Rosalynn Carter helped the mentally ill. Nancy Reagan fought drugs. It would make *you* look good — and the President, too — if you had a cause like those First Ladies."

While Chelsea pouted and Lane fumed, I looked at the newspaper. Suddenly, I got an idea.

"Hey, instead of *me* going to Florida to console the hurricane victims," I suggested, "why don't we send Chelsea?"

"Moon, that's brilliant!" Lane piped up.

"Ugh!" was Chelsea's response. "Hurricane victims are such a *downer*. And they're filthy. Why can't I go to Milan and comfort the victims of the spring fashion shows?"

"Don't you realize how dumb you seem?" Lane exploded. "The American people think you're a brainless, selfish airhead."

Chelsea just stared at Lane. I don't think anyone ever talked to her that way. She's so pretty and rich, people always let her get away with things that regular people couldn't, I guess. She looked shocked.

"What if I went down to Florida," she said meekly, "and delivered designer clothes to the hurricane victims?"

"You're kidding, right?" Lane asked, dumbfounded.

"Have you ever seen hurricane victims on TV?" Chelsea asked excitedly. "They look terrible, all dressed in rags. I'll go down there and deliver clothes to the people whose clothes blew away in the hurricane! Just because they have no homes is no reason they can't make themselves look good."

Lane and I looked at each other. It was a crazy idea, but we agreed that it had to be better than continuing to let Chelsea waste money on herself. Lane put her on the next plane to Florida.

Front page of The Washington Post, *June 30:*

MOON'S DAD RUNS BOX BIZ
FROM WHITE HOUSE!

16.
★ Mumbo-jumbo ★

As the months went by, I began to get used to the routine of being President. My days were busy, going from one appointment to the next.

Official luncheons. Receptions. Award ceremonies. Formal dinners. Classes with Miller the Killer. Doing my homework. Meeting with Vice-President Syers. Jogging with Secret Service Agent Doe. Shaking hands and shaking more hands. I shook so many hands that my right hand would throb and ache by the end of the day.

Is that all there is? I wondered as I sat at my desk in the Oval Office one morning. I had been President for eight months, but I still hadn't done anything important, anything that really mattered to the United States.

Oh, sure, I had fun at the annual Easter egg–rolling contest on the White House lawn. And throwing out the first ball to open baseball season at Camden Yards in Baltimore was really cool. But something was missing. Lane could tell I was feeling down when he came in for our usual morning meeting.

"Cheer up, Moon," he said. "You've lasted a *lot* longer than President William Henry Harrison."

"What happened to him?"

"Harrison was elected President in 1840," Lane said. "He was inaugurated in the pouring rain, then he caught a cold and died a month later."

That didn't make me feel any better.

"I want to do some *good* for this country," I told Lane. "I didn't accept this job just to get my picture taken."

"Well, you're going to *have* to do some good," Lane replied. "Did you see today's economic report?"

"No."

"The leading economic indicators are slipping," he said. "The consumer price index is up. Unemployment's up. Inflation's up. Housing starts are down. Retail sales are down. The stock market is down."

All that meant nothing to me. "You might as well be speaking Chinese," I said.

"The economy is on a downswing," Lane translated. "You've got to do something or your approval rating will take a downswing, too."

"Why do *I* have to fix the economy?" I asked. "I didn't break it."

"It doesn't matter," Lane replied. "You're in charge. And the American people care more about the economy than they do about *anything*. Crime, drugs, education, and the environment aren't as important to people as how much cash they have in their pockets."

The economy. I never understood what that meant, except it had something to do with money. It made no sense to me. All I knew was that the economy was doing great when I became President and everybody was happy. Now, suddenly, it wasn't so hot anymore and people were getting upset.

"What if I raise the minimum wage?" I suggested. "People will have more money to spend."

"Some people will," Lane agreed. "But the companies that pay those wages will have less money and they'll have to fire employees. Unemployment will go up, and that's bad."

"Then let's *lower* the minimum wage."

"If you do that, you'll throw millions of people into poverty," Lane said. "That's worse. You have to understand, Moon. Everything is connected with everything else. If the stock market goes up, the bond market goes down. If interest rates go down, inflation goes up."

By that time, my eyes had glazed over. Luckily, Vice-President Syers rolled in, pushed, as usual, by Chief Usher Honeywell. I was glad to see her, because if anybody could figure out this economic mumbo-jumbo, it was Vice-President Syers.

"Thank you, Roger," Mrs. Syers said sweetly as Honeywell locked the brake on her wheelchair.

"You are very welcome, Vice-President Syers," Honeywell replied as he left.

"Roger?" Lane asked Mrs. Syers. "Since when is Chief Usher Honeywell called Roger?"

"Ever since his mama named him," she snapped.

"Vice-President Syers," Lane said, "I'm sure you've seen the latest economic news. Have you got any solutions?"

"Boys," she said, "you're wastin' your time worryin' 'bout such nonsense."

"I beg your pardon?" Lane asked.

"Look, we got close to three hundred million people in this country," she explained. "If ya do one thing, fifty million of 'em'll hate ya. If ya do the opposite thing, fifty million others'll hate ya. If ya do something for the poor, the rich'll hate ya. If ya do something for the rich, the poor'll hate ya. If ya try to clean up the environment, business people'll hate ya. If you try to help business, environmental people'll hate ya. No matter what ya do to help somebody, it'll hurt somebody else, and they'll hate ya."

"So in other words," I said, "we should do nothing, because then nobody will hate us."

"I didn't say that," Mrs. Syers continued. "See, I got a plan that'll make everybody happy."

"What is it?" I asked, leaning toward her.

"It's simple," she whispered, as if she didn't want anyone else to hear. *"Make everything free."*

"Huh?" Lane asked.

"You heard me. *Free.* Don't sell nothin' no more. *Give* it all away."

Lane looked at Vice-President Syers like she was from another planet.

"Vice-President Syers," he said, "with all due respect, ma'am, if everything was free, how would the economy run? How would people provide for their families? How would anyone earn money to pay their bills?"

"If everything was free," Vice-President Syers explained, "nobody would *need* money. Nobody would *have* bills."

She had us there.

I still didn't understand the first thing about economics, or what I could do to help the nation's economy. But to tell you the truth, I'm not sure anybody else does, either.

THE PEOPLE SPEAK

★★★★★
"Do you approve or disapprove of the way President Moon is doing his job?"

58% Approve
35% Disapprove
7% Undecided

17.
Return of the
★ First Lady ★

When Chelsea returned from visiting the hurricane victims in Florida, I didn't really want to see her. I wasn't in the mood to hear about her designer clothes, her hair, the parties she wanted to throw, and all that other silliness she was always jabbering about.

When she walked into the Oval Office, I couldn't believe my eyes. Chelsea was wearing old gray sweatpants with a rip at one of the knees, cheap flip-flops, and a University of Florida T-shirt. Her hair wasn't carefully arranged. It was tied back in a ponytail with a rubber band. She wasn't wearing any makeup. She looked like a completely different person.

"Chelsea?" I asked, not completely convinced it was her. "Wh-where are your clothes?"

"Moon, I can't believe you would concern

yourself with clothes at a time like this," she scolded me. "I gave my clothes away. How could I think about clothes when the poor people of Florida don't even have a place to *live*?"

My mouth dropped open.

"And you *care*?" I asked, disbelieving.

"Moon, I've seen human suffering that you wouldn't believe," she said seriously. "I spoke with people who lost everything they had. I held in my arms babies who lost their parents. I met people who are living in rowboats. These people need help, Moon, and right away. I'm coordinating the rebuilding effort to get Florida back on its feet. From now on, that's all I care about."

"What about that dinner party tonight for the Miss America finalists?" I asked.

"I won't have time for hosting dinners or parties anymore, Moon. Life is short, and there are more important things to do."

She pulled a bunch of bills from her pocket and handed them to me.

"If you gave all your clothes away," I asked, "what are these for?"

"Food," she said. "Emergency medical supplies. Diapers. Books. Crutches. Wheelchairs."

Most people, I figure, don't change much over time. If they're good and honest people, it's not very likely that they'll suddenly turn mean and deceitful. Mean and deceitful people, I always assume, do not wake up one morning and suddenly become good and honest.

But people can change, and I suppose sometimes people can change dramatically. For the first time in her life, Chelsea must have seen something that shocked her to her senses. She must have realized that all her silly problems and the things she cared about were trivial compared with the *real* problems and concerns people in distress face.

For me, the resentment and anger I'd always felt toward Chelsea melted away instantly. Standing there in her ratty clothes, she seemed prettier than ever.

"I can't tell you how much this means to me," I said, "and to our country."

I felt a sudden overwhelming urge to give

Chelsea a hug and a kiss. I leaned toward her and closed my eyes.

I shouldn't have. She punched me in the nose.

"You're still a dork, Moon," she said. And then she walked out of the Oval Office.

18.
★ Hate and Love ★

When the press found out that Chelsea had devoted herself to helping the hurricane victims, she was ridiculed more than ever. One headline shouted:

CHELSEA CARES!
(YEAH, RIGHT!)

Another claimed:

FIRST LADY GIVES AWAY WARDROBE,
CLEARS CLOSET SPACE FOR NEW DUDS

Nobody believed that Chelsea genuinely cared about anyone but herself. They were sure that she was only *pretending* to care about the hurricane victims because she had been criticized for being selfish.

Many people believed that I had forced Chelsea to go to Florida so *I* would look good. Of course, if they knew Chelsea at all, they would know that I couldn't force her to do anything she didn't want to do.

Even if I *had* forced Chelsea to go to Florida, the strategy backfired. My approval rating was dropping like a rock. Every day there was another article saying I was weak, or stupid, or powerless, or spineless. The economy was in terrible shape, and people were really mad. Everything that went wrong was my fault. People would throw stuff at my limo as I drove by.

Any time of the night or day, I could look out the second floor windows at the White House and see the growing number of protesters at Lafayette Park across the street. They made huge banners to be sure I could read their messages: MOON IS A LIAR! I LOST MY JOB BECAUSE OF MOON! GO BACK TO 7TH GRADE! MOON IS A M-O-R-O-N!

"Get rid of Moon soon!" they'd chant, loud

enough to be heard from my window. "Get rid of Moon soon!"

Every day at exactly twelve o'clock, hundreds of people would stand shoulder to shoulder across the street from the White House. At a signal, they would turn their backs to me and shout, "Moon President Moon!" Then they'd all pull their pants down.

After a while, the daily "Noon Moon" got to be so annoying that I had all the shades in the White House pulled down just before twelve o'clock.

It seemed like only yesterday that I was on top of the world. America loved me. Everyone was so excited about having a young person lead the nation into the new millennium.

Now, according to the polls and what I saw across the street, it was just the opposite. I couldn't believe what was happening. I had to get a reality check.

Ladies and gentlemen, it said on computer screens all across America, welcome to the second Fireside Internet Chat with the President of the United States.

Hello America, I typed as "Hail to the Chief" came out of the speaker. I welcome your questions and comments.

A few seconds later, words came scrolling up the screen:

> PNUT: Moon sucks!
> JFISH: I hope you choke, Moon!
> MERRYMAN: Chuck a moon at Moon.
> ZZZTRANS: You let us down, you jerk!
> WANDA: I HATE YOU!!!!

Does anyone have any QUESTIONS? I typed.

> JACKNJILL: Yeah, when are you going to resign?
> ISCREAM: Whatever happened to your campaign promise to abolish homework?
> USCREAM: You're a fake and a phony.
> ROYJOY: Why don't you go back to school, little boy?

Does anyone have anything NICE to say? I typed.

> DRADA: No!
> NAIDECK: Yes, Hitler was a lot worse than you.

SPUTNIK: I love Chelsea.

I sighed as I shut down the computer. It was late and I was tired. I thought I'd ask Honeywell to bring me a little snack before I went to bed.

When I stepped out of the Oval Office, I gasped.

Honeywell was there, all right. But he wasn't alone. Vice-President Syers was with him. Honeywell was leaning over her wheelchair, and they were *kissing*!

I knew Honeywell and Vice-President Syers liked each other, but I didn't think they liked each other like *that*! I guess I never even thought old people kissed and stuff.

When he saw me looking at them, Honeywell quickly pulled himself away from Vice-President Syers. He looked very embarrassed.

"Uh, Mr. President," he stammered. "Can I get you anything before you retire for the evening, sir?"

"What are you two doing?" I asked, even though it was pretty obvious.

"What's it look like?" Vice-President Syers said. "We're neckin'!"

"I can't believe you're necking with a White House usher!"

"Why not?" she said. "I'm over eighty years old, and I'll neck with anyone I want!"

I couldn't argue with that. I just asked them to turn out the lights when they were through, and I went to bed.

19.
★ Grounded ★

As soon as Lane walked into the Oval Office, I knew something was up. His shoulders were a little stooped. He didn't have the usual spring in his step. He didn't look me in the eye.

"I suppose you saw today's paper," he sighed, tossing it on my desk. The headline read:

V.P. CAUGHT IN LOVE NEST
WITH WHITE HOUSE USHER!

"Moon," Lane continued, "I'm sorry."
"Sorry? For what? It's not your fault."
"I'm sorry about everything," Lane said. "I was supposed to guide you through the presidency. Help you. Protect you. If I had done my job well, none of these things would be in the papers. Your approval rating should be through

the roof. The people should love you. It's my fault. I let you down. I failed."

"Don't be ridiculous, Lane!" I argued. "You're doing the best job you can."

"It's not good enough," he said seriously. "I've given this a lot of thought, and I see only one way out of this mess."

He handed me a sheet of paper:

> *Dear President Moon,*
>   *Effective immediately, I resign my position as Chief of Staff to the President of the United States.*
>
>   *Sincerely,*
>   *Lane Brainard*

"You're *quitting*?!" I asked, my voice rising in panic.

"It's the only way, Moon," Lane replied softly.

"You can't quit!" I shouted. "I need you. How am I going to know what to do unless you tell me? I'm lost without you, Lane!"

"You'll be better off without me," he insisted.

"You're abandoning me!"

"I'm doing this for *you*, Moon," Lane said firmly. "Tell the press you fired me. Tell them I'm incompetent. They'll blame *me* for everything that's gone wrong. This will deflect the criticism away from you. I'm doing this to save your presidency, Moon. Part of the job of a presidential adviser is to protect the President."

"You protect the President by *quitting*?"

"Yes, if necessary."

I begged Lane to reconsider, but nothing I said would convince him to stay. When I realized that, I hugged Lane, we wished each other well, and he walked out of the Oval Office.

I would be on my own now until I got a new Chief of Staff. But how would I find anyone I trusted as much as I'd trusted Lane? I took a deep breath and went around behind my desk. I wasn't supposed to stand in front of the window for security reasons, but I didn't care. There were people out there. Tourists with cameras. Mothers with strollers. Groups of kids on school trips. Protesters exercising their freedom of speech.

Freedom. I envied them. Those people out there could say whatever they wanted. I couldn't. If I said one stupid thing, it would be on the front page of every newspaper in America the next day. The people outside could go wherever they wanted. I couldn't even go to a store and buy a candy bar without causing a riot.

Sure, the White House had a movie theater, a pool, video games, and a bowling alley. But I hardly ever had time to use them. And none of my friends were around to share them with me.

I thought about what my classmates back home were doing at that moment. They were at school, maybe at recess, playing basketball on the playground. I could hardly remember the last time I played basketball. I could hardly remember the last time I just *played*.

When school let out, they would ride their bikes home. They'd be hanging out at each other's houses, watching TV, playing video games, playing on sports teams, taking music lessons.

Then there were the kids who were being punished for one reason or another. They must be sitting in their rooms with nothing to do. They couldn't have any fun after school because they were grounded.

Being President of the United States, it seemed to me, was sort of like being grounded for four years.

I was miserable. Lane had resigned. Chelsea was off helping hurricane victims. I was a terrible President. And the public hated me. I had really *tried* to do good things for America, but from the moment I had been sworn into office everything just seemed to go wrong. Unless something incredible happened, my presidency was in deep trouble.

And then something incredible happened.

Front page of The Washington Post, *November 18:*

POPULARITY AT ALL-TIME LOW, MOON FIRES CHIEF OF STAFF

20.
Fireworks
★ in November ★

November 23 started out like most other days. I was being given a gift at the Four Seasons Hotel in Washington. Every year, just before Thanksgiving, the President is presented with a turkey.

They always pick a big turkey, because it shows up well in photos, which appear in lots of newspapers on Thanksgiving Day. This turkey was enormous — fifty-eight pounds. The thing was way too big for anybody to eat. After the photographers were done, I was told, I would receive a regular turkey and they'd send the big one back to the farm where it came from.

"Keep an eye on that turkey," I instructed Secret Service Agent Doe when the turkey was led away. "It looks like it might have a bomb inside it."

"Yes, sir," he replied. I had been trying to make Doe laugh ever since I became President, but so far I had been unsuccessful.

As we left the hotel I was surrounded, as always, by Secret Service agents. Agent Doe was in the front, while eight or nine other agents walked by my side and behind me.

My limousine was parked on the street by the side entrance to the hotel. The Secret Service doesn't like to pull up to a front entrance because too many people gather around to catch a glimpse of me and it can be difficult to control the crowd.

The limo was about fifteen feet from the door. As I walked out the door, I could see some reporters and photographers gathered behind a rope, along with a few curious passersby. I waved to them and shouted greetings.

I was about halfway to the limo when I heard a popping sound.

Pop . . . poppop. Pop. It sounded like those little firecrackers my friends and I used to set off on the Fourth of July. There was a burst of about five or six pops. For a moment the thought crossed my mind that Thanksgiving was an odd time to be setting off fireworks.

I was still waving to the crowd when Agent Doe stumbled in front of me and then tumbled to the sidewalk.

"Are you okay?" I started to ask him. I bent down to see what was wrong, but suddenly one of the other Secret Service agents grabbed me from behind and threw his body over me.

"Hey, get off!" I yelled.

"Get the President out of here!" somebody yelled. "Get him out!"

There was wild confusion after that. People started screaming and running around. Agent Doe was writhing on the sidewalk. There was a red splotch on his white shirt.

Somebody picked me up, threw me into the limo, and jumped on top of me. I made sure I still had the football. There was a siren. And just a few seconds after I first heard the popping sound, the tires screeched and the limo sped off.

"George Washington University Hospital," one of the Secret Service agents barked to the driver.

"What's going on?" I asked when the other agent got off me.

"Somebody tried to shoot you, sir."

"I think Agent Doe might have been hit!" I yelled. "We've got to go back and get him!"

"No, sir," one of the agents told me. "Our job is to protect *you.*"

I didn't think I was hit. They searched me for bullet holes. They didn't find any but insisted on taking me to the hospital just to be on the safe side. If it hadn't been for Agent Doe walking in front of me, I realized, that would have been *me* bleeding on the sidewalk.

On the way to the hospital, we got word by cell phone that a man had been arrested. He had a history of mental problems and had managed to get a gun and position himself with the group of reporters who were waiting for me as I came out of the hotel.

"What about Agent Doe?" I shouted.

"They're rushing him to George Washington University Hospital," was the response.

We were at the hospital in minutes. I ran ahead of the Secret Service agents and rushed through the automatic doors of the emergency room. The guard told me the ambulance hadn't arrived yet.

"His name is John Doe!" I shouted to the lady at the admissions desk. "And that's his real name! He's a big guy. Black. Bald. You've got to save his life!"

A few seconds later, the ambulance pulled up, sirens blaring. Two paramedics dashed outside and began to unload the stretcher. They struggled to carry Agent Doe's enormous body, so my Secret Service agents and I ran over to help. There was blood all over Doe's shirt now.

"Hang on!" I yelled at him as we rolled him inside. "Don't die on me."

Agent Doe didn't respond. His eyes were closed. I couldn't tell whether or not he was breathing.

I held the handrail of the stretcher as we pushed it down the corridor. I kept saying encouraging things, but Agent Doe wasn't responding. We came to a set of big double doors.

"We'll take it from here, Mr. President," a nurse said.

"But I want to be with him," I protested.

"I'm sorry, sir," she told me. "You're not allowed in the operating room."

I sat in the waiting room with the Secret Service agents for the next three hours. Every so often I'd get up and ask a nurse if she had any information about Agent Doe. All she could tell me was that she would let me know as soon as she got a report.

I skimmed a magazine, but I couldn't pay attention to the words. I kept thinking about Agent Doe.

Finally, a doctor came out and walked straight toward me. I was prepared for the worst.

"Agent Doe is alive," he said.

I let out a big sigh of relief. "Is he going to be okay?" I asked.

"He took a pretty good hit, sir," the doctor continued. "The human body has five to six quarts of blood in it, and he's lost quite a bit. We're replacing it, and he's in stable condition. There's no blood in his stomach, which is good."

"Where was he hit?" I asked.

"We found three .22 caliber bullets in him. None of them hit his heart, but one entered below his left arm, traveled down about three inches, struck his seventh rib, and lodged itself in his lung. There is no exit wound."

"What does that mean?"

"It means the bullet is still inside him. But that's okay. Lots of people live their whole lives with bullets in them. He's a big fellow. I think he's going to make it, sir."

The last time I cried, I was in third grade. We had planted some seeds in paper cups, and mine was the only one that didn't grow. The other kids in the class made so much fun of me for crying that I resolved never to let anyone see me cry again.

But I was so sad that Agent Doe had been shot, and so happy that he was still alive, that I couldn't hold back my tears.

Later, Agent Doe was wheeled out to the recovery room and I got to see him. There were tubes going in and out of different parts of his body and a clear plastic mask was over his nose and mouth. Plastic bags filled with liquid hung over his bed. He was hooked up to some machines, I guess to help him breathe.

I had always thought of Agent Doe as a big, tough guy. But now, lying there helplessly in a green surgical gown, he looked so weak. It's amazing what a tiny bullet can do to a human body. I took his huge hand in mine.

Agent Doe's eyes were shut when he was wheeled into the recovery room, but soon the drugs wore off and his eyelids flickered open. He couldn't speak because of all the tubes. He saw me and signaled with his hands that he wanted to write something on a piece of paper. The doctor indicated it was okay, and I handed Doe a pad and pencil.

R U OK? he wrote, grimacing with pain.

"I'm fine," I replied. "How about you?"

BEEN BETTER.

"Now we're even," I told him. "I saved your life when you were in the pool, and you saved mine today."

JUST DOING MY JOB, he wrote.

A nurse came into the room. He was holding a special afternoon edition of *The Washington Post*, and he held it up for Agent Doe to see the headline:

SECRET SERVICE AGENT IS HERO, TAKES BULLETS AIMED AT MOON

Next to the story of the shooting was the usual approval rating nonsense:

THE PEOPLE SPEAK

★★★★★

"Do you approve or disapprove of the way President Moon is doing his job?"

77% Approve

15% Disapprove

8% Undecided

"Wow," I said, "I haven't been *this* popular since the inauguration."

U SHOULD GET SHOT AT EVERY DAY, Agent Doe wrote on his pad.

"Is that a *joke*?" I asked him. "Did you *actually* tell a *joke*? I can't believe it!" I started yelling to all who could hear, "Agent Doe told a joke! Alert the media! Stop the presses! This should be front page news! Declare a national holiday!"

STOP IT, he wrote. HURTS TO LAUGH.

"You're *laughing*?!"

I grabbed my chest and pretended to fall down in a dead faint.

"Agent Doe is actually laughing!" I hollered to the nurses. "I can't believe it. Somebody get a camcorder! I need to get this on video to pre- serve for future generations! Nobody will ever believe it."

STOP! he wrote again, underlining the word.

With all those tubes going in and out of him, I can't say for sure that Agent Doe was laughing. But his body was shaking, he had a big smile on his face, and tears were sliding down his cheeks. That was good enough for me.

The worst crisis of my presidency was over. Or so I thought.

21.
The Christmas
★ Surprise ★

Every year, a tree is chosen to be the national Christmas tree. It is brought to Washington and displayed on the White House lawn. This year's tree was a huge evergreen that grew in Pennsylvania. It was a beautiful thing, decorated with ornaments made by children from all the fifty states.

I got to ride a cherry picker to place a star on the top of the tree. Then I flicked the switch that turned on the lights. The whole world seemed to brighten. A choir sang Christmas carols until midnight. Just as they launched into "White Christmas," snow began to fall. It was a magical evening.

My first year in office was almost over. In a few weeks, I would be giving the annual State of the Union Address. I certainly hadn't been the best President in American history, but I hadn't been the worst, either. My approval rating was very high after the assassination attempt. I was a survivor, in more ways than one. Things had gone pretty well, all in all.

On Christmas Eve, I went to bed thinking about the presents my parents were going to give me in the morning. I had my eye on a new video game system and hoped I'd dropped enough hints so they would buy it for me.

I was in the middle of a deep sleep when I felt someone shaking me.

"Santa?" I grunted hopefully. "Is that you?"

"Mr. President, wake up, sir. It's important."

It was Honeywell. He was with Vice-President Syers.

"Too early," I muttered. "Leave me alone."

"President Moon," Vice-President Syers said urgently, "there are troops on the border of Cantania, and they look like they're going to invade Boraguay. You've got to get up right away."

"Just nuke them," I said groggily, "and let me go back to sleep."

"This is a national emergency!" Vice-President Syers said as she pulled off my covers. "Get up!"

I rubbed the sleep from my eyes, throwing on a bathrobe and my fuzzy slippers. The clock next to my bed said it was two in the morning. I accompanied Vice-President Syers down to the Map Room in the basement of the White House. Some men in military uniform were seated around the long table — the Secretary of Defense, the Chairman of the Joint Chiefs of Staff, Brigadier General Herbert Dunn, and Colonel Dwaine Cooper of the Air Force.

I hadn't had the chance to spend much time with the leaders of the armed forces during my first eleven months as President. But when I walked into the room, they all snapped to attention and saluted.

"What's up?" I asked, returning their salutes.

"Mr. President," the Secretary of Defense said, "our spy satellites have detected — and we have photographic proof — that in South America the Cantanian army is massing at the border of Boraguay. We believe an invasion will come within the next twenty-four hours."

"Why is that our business?" I asked. "If two countries want to fight, why should we stop them?"

"Because Boraguay is one of the biggest oil-producing nations in the world, sir. Their government is friendly to the United States. If Cantania takes over the oil fields, the United States will be at the mercy of Supreme Ruler Raul Trujillo, the dictator who runs Cantania."

"Trujillo . . . Trujillo . . ." I mumbled. "How do I know that name?"

"He was at your first state dinner," Vice-President Syers reminded me.

"Oh yeah," I recalled. "The *friendly* dictator. He seemed drunk or something."

"He's drunk with power," the Chairman of the Joint Chiefs of Staff said. "We've got to stop him, sir."

"What do you suggest we do?" I asked.

"I say we attack now," General Dunn said, pounding the table. "Bomb them back to the Stone Age. Teach 'em a lesson."

"Yes, and start World War III!" snorted Colonel Cooper. "We have to be very cautious, sir. I suggest we cut off all relations with Cantania immediately."

"That makes us look weak!" General Dunn insisted. "We've got to let Trujillo know we'll use our military might if we have to."

"We could blockade them," the Secretary of Defense said. "That's what Kennedy did to end the Cuban Missile Crisis in 1962. We could cut off all food and supplies entering Cantania."

"It's too late for that," commented Vice-President Syers.

"Why not consult Congress?" I suggested. "Let them debate the issue and then make a decision."

"There's no time, sir! Trujillo will have the manpower and supplies to launch an attack by late tomorrow."

"If we bomb them, we don't have to call it a war, you know," General Dunn said. "Call it a police action. That's what Truman did in Korea in 1950. We never officially declared war in Vietnam or the Persian Gulf, either."

The four of them discussed all the options the United States could take. When they were done, they all looked at me.

The final decision, I realized, was mine. These military leaders couldn't make this decision for me. Congress couldn't make this decision for me. My *parents* couldn't make this decision for me.

When I first became President, I had complained that the President didn't have the power to do much. But now I was facing a situation in which I had enormous power. My decision would affect the course of world history. It was terrifying.

As I sat there with all their eyes trained on me, I felt like saying, "What are you guys looking at *me* for? I'm just a kid."

"How long do I have to reach a decision?" I asked the group.

"We need to send a clear message to Trujillo first thing in the morning, sir," said the Secretary of Defense.

"Gentlemen," I said, saluting them, "then I'll see you here first thing in the morning."

I pushed Vice-President Syers' wheelchair out

of the Map Room. Honeywell said he would escort her home.

"Some Christmas present, huh?" Vice-President Syers said as she rolled down the ramp to her car.

22.
★ Strength ★

Going back to sleep was out of the question. I had just been informed that I had five hours to make a decision that could plunge the United States into a foreign war. How could I sleep?

A long hallway runs the entire length of the second floor of the White House. All was quiet as I paced back and forth in my bathrobe and fuzzy slippers. Mom and Dad's room was silent. So was Chelsea's room and her parents' room. The Secret Service agents were out of sight. Honeywell hadn't returned yet from driving Vice-President Syers home. For once, I had the whole White House to myself.

And then I heard a noise.

It sounded like a bed creaking, or maybe a floorboard. I turned. There it was again! It was coming from the Lincoln Bedroom. My dad must be working late, I figured, filling orders for the White House Box and Carpet Tile Company.

I opened the door gently and let out a gasp. There, sitting calmly on the bed, was Abraham Lincoln.

It couldn't be the real Abraham Lincoln, I knew. Lincoln was cut down by an assassin's bullet in 1865. It had to be his ghost. Honeywell told me the ghost of Abraham Lincoln had been spotted in the White House, and I had living proof of it. Well, *proof* of it, anyway. The ghost looked more like a hologram than a live person.

When I opened the door, Lincoln turned his head and looked at me. He didn't look exactly like the Abraham Lincoln on a five-dollar bill. He appeared younger. There were fewer lines in his face. Death had been good to him.

"It is time we met," Lincoln said softly. "The Union is in crisis. It is the eternal struggle between these two principles — right and wrong. They are the two principles that have stood face to face from the beginning of time and will ever continue to struggle."

"Y-yes," I croaked. "Sorry about all the boxes

and stuff. This is my dad's home office. He didn't know you would —"

"Never mind that," Lincoln interrupted. "What course of action do you intend to take?" Clearly, Lincoln was not in the mood for chitchat.

"I don't know," I admitted. "I've always done what people told me to do. I'm just a boy."

"Now you must lead, as a man," Lincoln said. "The presidency is like a suit. Many try it on. Sometimes it fits. Sometimes not. And sometimes . . . one grows into it. I was a simple country lawyer before I tried on that suit. I had to grow into it. So must you."

"I'm prepared to lead," I said, "but I don't want to lead America to war."

"Neither did I," Lincoln said sadly. "War came to me. I could not escape it. Perhaps you can."

"How?"

"That I do not know," Lincoln sighed. "But I beg you to remember this. The government should not use force unless force is used against it. In a choice of evils, war may not always be the worst. Still, I would do all in my power to avert it. As Commander in Chief, you have the right to take any measure that will preserve the Union, subdue an enemy, and ultimately bring peace. I was successful in achieving those goals. But the price — six hundred thousand lives — was enormous. I pray the mighty scourge of war may speedily pass away. I must take my leave."

"Wait!" I shouted. "What would you do if you were in my shoes?"

"Use your strength," Lincoln said. Then he looked down at my fuzzy slippers with a half smile. "And get new shoes."

With that, Abraham Lincoln faded away.

What did he mean when he said, "Use your strength"? I wondered as I went back to my room. Was he suggesting I use the strength of the United States military against Trujillo? Or was he saying I should use my strength to lead the nation out of this crisis and avoid going to war? Why are ghosts always so ambiguous?

In the hour or two of sleep I got that night, I realized that Lincoln meant something entirely different. When I woke up, I had settled on the strategy I would take with Trujillo.

23.
★ A People Person ★

The crisis had already hit the morning papers by sunrise. **TRUJILLO POISED TO INVADE BORAGUAY,** screamed a big headline in *The Washington Post*. **MOON WEIGHS OPTIONS.**

The four military leaders were waiting for me when I arrived at the Map Room at seven A.M. For all I knew, they had been there all night. Vice-President Syers wheeled herself in shortly after me. There was obvious tension in the air.

"Good morning," I said, snapping off a crisp salute to the generals. "Is there any change in the situation?"

"No, sir," the Secretary of Defense reported. "Our satellites show Trujillo's army is still massing at the border. It's almost as if he's waiting to see how we respond, sir."

"He won't have to wait much longer," I informed the group. "I've made my decision."

"To attack?" General Dunn asked hopefully.

"No," I replied. "I want to meet with Trujillo. Face to face. Man to man. Alone."

The generals let out a collective gasp.

"Alone?" Colonel Cooper asked, as if he hadn't heard me correctly.

"Alone," I repeated. "No generals. No weapons. No nothing."

"That's insanity!" the Secretary of Defense exclaimed.

"This is crazy! He's just a boy," scoffed General Dunn, standing up to address the group. "What does he know about handling a military crisis?"

"I know one thing," I said, raising my voice slightly. "I know that I'm the President. If you can't deal with that, you can turn in your resignation right now, General Dunn."

Vice-President Syers looked at me approvingly. The general sat back down and kept his mouth shut.

"Sir," the Secretary of Defense said, more respectfully. "For you to meet with Trujillo would be very dangerous. He's a madman." The other military leaders nodded their heads in agreement.

"But he's a man," I replied. "Look, I know it's dangerous. I considered the options you proposed. We could bomb Cantania. We could blockade them. We could cut off all relations with them. All these options have their problems. I have no guarantee that my idea will work. But we're going to try it first."

"I'm not sure your plan is constitutional, sir," the Secretary of Defense said.

"Maybe not," I snapped. "But this is a national emergency. I'm using the Executive Power that's granted to the President only in a time of emergency."

Vice-President Syers raised an eyebrow, impressed that I had remembered what she'd told me.

"Send a message to Trujillo that I want to meet with him immediately," I continued. "If he chooses not to meet with me and advances his troops over the Boraguay border, I want you to bomb Cantania back to the Stone Age."

"Yes, sir!" the Secretary of Defense said.

The generals went scurrying off to arrange a meeting with Trujillo. I pushed Vice-President Syers' wheelchair to the elevator. We rode it up to the second floor and she rolled alongside me to the Oval Office.

"If anything happens to me," I told her solemnly, "I'm sure you'll make a fine President."

"You sure you know what you're doin', Moon?" Vice-President Syers asked.

"No," I answered honestly. "But remember when you used to baby-sit for me and I would talk you into letting me stay up past my bedtime?"

"Yeah."

"And I would talk you into giving me an extra dessert or more video game time?"

"You could just about talk the paint off a wall, Moon," she chuckled.

"Well, I was always able to get what I wanted by just talking," I said. "I'm a people person. That's how I won the election. So I figured I should use my strength and meet with Trujillo one on one."

"How'd you come up with that crazy idea?" she asked.

"Let's just say it came to me in the middle of the night," I replied.

I rolled Vice-President Syers back down the hallway and then down the ramp outside the White House. She was unusually quiet, as if she had something to say but wasn't sure if she wanted to tell me.

"What is it?" I asked.

"I made a big decision last night, too," she said, embarrassed. "When this whole mess blows over, Chief Usher Honeywell and I are gonna get married. He proposed yesterday."

I wrapped my arms around Vice-President Syers and gave her a big hug.

"So don't go blowin' up the world now, y'hear?" she warned, pointing a finger at me. "'Cause that would really louse up my honeymoon."

Front page of The Washington Post, *December 26:*

MAN TO ... MAN?
MOON TO CONFRONT TRUJILLO

24.
Meeting with
★ a Madman ★

Air Force One is a beautiful plane. It's a modi-fied 747, blue and white, with the words UNITED STATES OF AMERICA running along each side. The American flag is painted on the tail.

On both sides of the jet's nose is the presidential seal — an eagle holding arrows in one claw and an olive branch in the other. The arrows represent war and the olive branch represents peace. The eagle is facing the olive branch.

When I said good-bye to my parents at Andrews Air Force Base, I wasn't sure I would ever see them again. I could return home a hero, or I could return home as the President who started World War III. Or maybe I would return home in a casket. When I hugged my mom, she didn't want to let go. Neither did I.

Vice-President Syers couldn't come with

me on *Air Force One*. The President and Vice-President are not allowed to fly in the same plane. *Ever.* If the plane crashed, the government would be in disarray. As always, I kept the football with me at all times.

Under different circumstances, I could have had a really great time on *Air Force One*. It's probably the only plane in the world that has a bed, a lounge, desks, sofas, and two kitchens. As soon as the President takes his seat, the plane starts rolling down the runway. You don't have to wait a minute. And the food is a lot better than those crummy bags of peanuts they give you on regular planes.

But I couldn't enjoy any of that. I was thinking about Trujillo. What could I say to him to make him change his mind about invading Boraguay? I didn't know. I just felt in my bones that if I could sit down with the man and look him in the eye, I could talk him out of doing something crazy.

Trujillo had agreed to meet with me but not in the United States. I told him I wouldn't meet him in Cantania. I suggested a neutral location — a cruise ship in the Atlantic—and he agreed. We both agreed to arrive with no body-guards, no advisers, and no weapons.

Air Force One landed at a United States naval base in Brazil. From there, I took a helicopter to the *Horizon*, a Swedish cruise ship off the coast of Argentina.

I arrived first. The captain of the *Horizon* greeted me warmly and led me to the room where Trujillo and I would be meeting. He left me alone there.

The room was nearly bare, with just two chairs and a table with a pitcher of water and two glasses on it. There was an intercom that would let us call the captain if we needed anything. I felt around the drapes to make sure there weren't any hidden listening devices. When I was satisfied, I sat down, put the football on the table, and rehearsed what I was going to say to Trujillo.

He showed up a few minutes later, escorted by the captain. Trujillo was wearing a military uniform with lots of ribbons and medals dangling off it like Christmas tree ornaments. They didn't impress me.

"So we meet again, President Moon," Trujillo

said, a cocky tone in his voice. He didn't stick out his hand, and neither did I.

"Lock the door," I instructed the captain. "We're not coming out of this room until we reach an agreement."

With the room sealed, Trujillo and I stood face to face. He was a short man but was still a few inches taller than me.

"It is time to separate the men from the boys, President Moon," he sneered. "I could just kill you now. Do you realize that?"

"Mr. Trujillo," I said, "I didn't come here to separate anything. I came here to bring us together."

"Bring us together? Ha!" he snorted. "You only came here to protect your precious oil. Without your planes and guns and bombs —"

"Forget about planes and guns and bombs," I interrupted. "I have a proposal for you. A simple proposal. Either listen to what I have to say, or the United States will take military action against Cantania."

"What proposal could you possibly have that would interest me?"

"I always thought it was stupid that soldiers

have to die in wars when it's the rulers who have disagreements," I explained. "Wouldn't it make more sense if the leaders of the two nations simply fought it out between themselves?"

"Are you suggesting that you and I fight?" Trujillo said with a laugh.

"Yes!" I said. "You and I fight. Right here in this room. If you win, you can go ahead and invade Boraguay. America won't interfere. And if I win, you pull back your troops and never bother the people of Boraguay again. Either way, no bombs are dropped. No bullets are fired. Nobody has to die."

"Good," he said, rolling up his sleeves. "Instead of fighting a war, we will arm wrestle."

"No," I said. "You're obviously much stronger than me. It has to be a fair fight."

"Guns," Trujillo suggested.

"No."

"Swords, then."

"No."

"What, then?" he asked.

"Video games," I replied. "I'm suggesting that instead of a real war, you and I have a virtual war to settle our differences."

Trujillo looked me over carefully, jamming his hands into his pockets.

"Do you take me for a fool?" he asked. "Video games are a children's toy. That is no more fair to me than arm wrestling is to you."

"That's my offer," I replied. "Take it or leave it."

"Why do *you* get to choose weapons?" he asked.

"Because I've got all those planes and guns and bombs," I replied. "And I'm not afraid to use them."

Trujillo thought over my proposal for a few seconds.

"I will play a video game against you," he said, "on one condition — I choose the game."

"Agreed," I quickly said. We shook hands for the first time, to seal the deal.

"We will play *this* game," he said, as he reached into his pocket and pulled out a Nintendo cartridge. The label read, WORLD WAR FOUR.

"What's that?" I asked.

"A video game," Trujillo replied. "It belongs to my twelve-year-old son. He plays it so much that I took it away from him this morning."

"I never heard of that game," I said. Suddenly, the room was feeling warm and my forehead was sweating. I didn't even know they *had* video games in Cantania.

"This game was made by a Cantanian game designer," Trujillo said with a smile. "A friend of mine. It is not available anywhere else in the world. I think you will enjoy playing it, President Moon."

"Have you played this game with your son?" I asked.

"For many hours," he replied. "I have become quite good at it, actually."

I gulped.

Front page of The Washington Post, *December 28:*

THE WORLD WAITS WHILE MOON, TRUJILLO MEET SECRETLY

25.
★ Virtual War ★

I'm quite good at video games, actually. Once I learn the ins and outs of a game, I can beat just about anybody. Certainly any *grown-up*. My dad tried to play me a few times, and he was totally pathetic. Trujillo probably wasn't any better.

But I was rusty. I hadn't had the chance to play any video games since the election. And if Trujillo had played World War Four with his son and was good at it, he could be tough to beat.

If I lost the game, I knew, my presidency would be a failure. The newspapers would eat me alive. I felt incredible pressure to win.

I also felt like an idiot. Trujillo had tricked me into playing his video game. It was too late to back out. After all, playing a video game had been my idea in the first place.

I pushed a button on the intercom and asked

the captain to bring us a Nintendo system and a TV set. He sounded surprised by the request but said he would get whatever we needed.

A few minutes later, a guy opened the door and wheeled in a cart with the equipment. As he was setting it up, he stole a few curious glances at Trujillo and me. Then he left and locked the door behind him. Trujillo put his cartridge in, flipped the ON switch, and World War Four appeared on the screen.

According to the designer of this game, World War Four will be fought between the two superpowers left after World War Three — The United States and Cantania. North America and South America appear on a split screen, showing the two continents side by side.

"What's the object of the game?" I asked as I picked up a controller.

"Total nuclear annihilation."

"You have nukes, too?" I asked.

"But of course," Trujillo replied with a smile. "It would not be a fair fight if one side had an advantage, would it, President Moon?"

He was looking at me with a grin so big I could see his yellowed teeth. All his life, I guessed, Trujillo had hated and feared the power of the United States. Now his nation was an equal to mine, at least on-screen. He was loving it.

Both nations had an arsenal of a hundred nuclear missiles. Some of them could be dropped from airplanes, others launched from submarines, and some could be fired from the ground. Each player also had a nuclear defense shield — sort of an umbrella you could move around the screen to stop incoming missiles before they hit the ground. The buttons on the controller were used to launch missiles, and the joystick moved the shield around.

The idea was simple — wipe your opponent's country off the face of the earth before he does the same to yours. This game would *not* win any Parent's Choice Awards for software that is good for kids.

"Shall we begin, President Moon?"

"A warm-up game would be sporting," I said.

"As you wish," Trujillo agreed. "That will allow me to destroy America *twice*."

Trujillo hit his START button and immediately fired ten nukes from his submarines off the Atlantic and Pacific coasts. Red lines on the screen showed flight paths as the missiles made their way toward American soil. I barely had a chance to blink when Trujillo launched ten more nukes from his bombers streaking across the sky.

Missiles were coming in from all directions. I rushed to defend my biggest cities — New York, Los Angeles, and Chicago—plus Washington, D.C. My shield stopped most of the nukes that were heading for those places, but I couldn't stop every one. Trujillo started hitting targets in the smaller cities. Ankeny, Iowa, was wiped out in one shot. I lost Hilliard, Ohio; Bibb County, Alabama; and Fayetteville, North Carolina.

When each nuke hit a target, the area for miles around would turn gray, the color of ashes. That meant it was contaminated by nuclear fallout and declared uninhabitable.

"Death to America!" Trujillo yelled when Spring, Texas, was incinerated.

I went to stop the nukes that were heading for the smaller cities, but then Trujillo began aiming for the bigger ones. Quickly, I lost Philadelphia, St. Louis, Houston, San Francisco, and Baltimore. The map of America was turning gray.

"Just like I told you," Trujillo shouted gleefully, "without a military advantage, my country can crush yours like an insect!"

"It's not over yet," I shot back. But in short order I lost Boston and Los Angeles. My situation was hopeless. When Trujillo sneaked a nuke past my shield and wiped out Washington, a huge mushroom cloud rose over America and the whole country turned a sickly gray.

GAME OVER, the screen said as the Cantania national anthem played. THE UNITED STATES HAS BEEN DESTROYED. CANTANIA RULES THE WORLD.

I slammed my fist against the table. I hadn't had the chance to fire a single missile.

"*Hahahahahahaha!*" Trujillo chortled triumphantly. "Victory is joyous!"

"Hit the reset button," I said tersely.

26.
★ World War Four ★

"Why so serious, President Moon?" Trujillo smirked after he had reduced the United States to a pile of rubble. "It's only a *game*."

"Shut up and play," I said. "This time it counts."

For all I knew, Trujillo might have had the game programmed so that America would *always* lose. I wouldn't put it past him.

But I couldn't worry about that. Clearly, the strategy I used in the practice game didn't work. I had to come up with something different, or Trujillo would destroy me just as easily again. And I had to think of a better strategy fast.

It occurred to me that because the United States was so large, it was impossible to defend *all* of it from incoming missiles. Cantania was a the goalie on a bad hockey team, stopping shot after shot on goal. He couldn't keep it up forever, I figured. At some point, one of my shots would have to make it through.

With just a few remaining nukes on the screen, one of them did get through. It was a sub-based missile I had launched from pretty far out in the Atlantic. Trujillo ignored it so he could stop my other missiles, and by the time he got his shield back to stop this one, it was too late.

"Go, baby!" I shouted.

The missile missed his shield by a pixel or two and crashed into Cantania. A big mushroom cloud rose over the country.

GAME OVER, the screen read, as the American national anthem played. CANTANIA HAS BEEN DESTROYED. THE UNITED STATES RULES THE WORLD.

I relaxed in my chair, exhausted from concentrating so hard. I looked over at Trujillo for the first time since the game began. He was sweating and breathing heavily. He threw down his controller in disgust.

"Good game," I said.

I pressed the intercom button and notified the captain that Supreme Ruler Trujillo and I had

tiny country, about the size of Rhode Island. It was easy for Trujillo to defend his land.

Thinking it over some more, I realized that America's size also gave me an advantage. I could afford to lose ten, twenty, even thirty large cities and still stay alive. But if I could land just one or two nukes on little Cantania, I might be able to wipe out the whole country.

I decided to attack.

When Trujillo pushed the START button this time, I already had my finger on my LAUNCH button. I fired off ten nukes from my subs, another ten from my planes, and ten more from my ground-based launchers. I was pressing the LAUNCH button as fast as I could.

Trujillo had only gotten off a few shots when he saw thirty of my nuclear missiles heading for Cantania. If just a few of them reached the ground, he would lose the game right then and there. He had no choice but to stop firing at me and devote his energy to defending his country.

He was good. He zipped his shield around the screen expertly, picking off my missiles just before they would have hit the ground.

Every so often he would manage to get off a shot at the United States. I ignored his missiles. I just kept firing. Playing aggressively, I had the upper hand, and he knew it.

"You learn fast, President Moon," Trujillo said as he stopped another one of my missiles. "But Cantania will still prevail."

He was trying to distract me. I kept firing. The screen was filled with nukes heading for Cantania.

A little counter at the top of the screen indicated how many missiles each of us had left. Trujillo still had almost all his missiles. My counter was already down below fifty and falling with every push of my trigger.

It occurred to me that if I couldn't get through Trujillo's defenses soon, I would run out of ammo. Then he could go on the attack, easily picking off American cities one at a time.

Still, I stayed with my strategy. Every time he stopped one of my nukes, I launched three more. Trujillo's planes were just circling around with nothing to do. He had to use all his concentration to defend Cantania.

Finally, I managed to get one nuke past him,

and half of Cantania turned gray. One more good shot and the game would be mine.

After five minutes, I had only ten nukes left — three in my submarines, three in my bombers, and four in my ground-based launchers. I could have fired them one at a time, rotating them to try and confuse Trujillo. But he was so fast with his shield. I decided to just let them all fly in one all-out, last-ditch attack.

I pushed the button and breathed a sigh of relief as the missiles left their bases. From my point of view, my game was over. If one of my nukes hit the target, I would win the game. If Trujillo stopped them all, he would win. It was out of my hands. I hit the trigger one last time just to make sure I was out of ammo. Nothing happened. My missiles were all gone.

I'm not sure if Trujillo noticed that I had stopped firing. He was concentrating heavily on the screen. Those last ten nukes were streaking toward Cantania, plus ten or twenty I had fired earlier.

Trujillo flicked his shield around the screen blocking my nukes milliseconds before they would have reached their targets. He was completed our negotiations. Almost immediately, the door opened.

"Captain," I said calmly as I picked up my briefcase, "Mr. Trujillo and I have resolved our differences. Please notify our respective governments. There is no need for us to go to war. No need for soldiers to die. The crisis is over. Cantania's forces will retreat."

"Never!" Trujillo shouted. Suddenly, he came up behind me and grabbed me around the neck so his forearm was wrapped tightly around my windpipe.

"Give me the football!" he shouted in my ear.

"What football?" I choked. "I don't have a football."

"The briefcase with your nuclear codes!" he yelled. "Give it to me or I will kill you."

I let go of the briefcase and he took it with his other hand.

"That's a good boy," Trujillo said, keeping a firm grip on my throat.

"Mr. President!" the captain exclaimed.

"Make one move and the President is dead!" Trujillo shouted at the captain. "I control the President of the United States and its nuclear arsenal. How does it feel, President Moon? Without your planes and guns and bombs, the United States is powerless."

"The minute you walk out of this room you'll be killed," I choked out.

"I'm not afraid to die!" Trujillo gloated. "Can you say the same, President Moon? Because you're going to be my human shield until we get back to Cantania. There I will parade you through the streets for the entertainment of my people."

"We had a deal," I choked.

"Did you really think I was going to give up because you beat me in a *video game*?" Trujillo laughed. "Foolish boy."

How stupid I was! How could I allow myself to be alone in a room with a ruthless dictator and no Secret Service agents to protect me in case he tried anything?

At that moment the image of Agent John Doe flashed through my mind. He was still in the hospital after the attempt on my life. If only Doe were here, he would kick Trujillo's butt.

Wait!

tiny country, about the size of Rhode Island. It was easy for Trujillo to defend his land.

Thinking it over some more, I realized that America's size also gave me an advantage. I could afford to lose ten, twenty, even thirty large cities and still stay alive. But if I could land just one or two nukes on little Cantania, I might be able to wipe out the whole country.

I decided to attack.

When Trujillo pushed the START button this time, I already had my finger on my LAUNCH button. I fired off ten nukes from my subs, another ten from my planes, and ten more from my ground-based launchers. I was pressing the LAUNCH button as fast as I could.

Trujillo had only gotten off a few shots when he saw thirty of my nuclear missiles heading for Cantania. If just a few of them reached the ground, he would lose the game right then and there. He had no choice but to stop firing at me and devote his energy to defending his country.

He was good. He zipped his shield around the screen expertly, picking off my missiles just before they would have hit the ground.

Every so often he would manage to get off a shot at the United States. I ignored his missiles. I just kept firing. Playing aggressively, I had the upper hand, and he knew it.

"You learn fast, President Moon," Trujillo said as he stopped another one of my missiles. "But Cantania will still prevail."

He was trying to distract me. I kept firing. The screen was filled with nukes heading for Cantania.

A little counter at the top of the screen indicated how many missiles each of us had left. Trujillo still had almost all his missiles. My counter was already down below fifty and falling with every push of my trigger.

It occurred to me that if I couldn't get through Trujillo's defenses soon, I would run out of ammo. Then he could go on the attack, easily picking off American cities one at a time.

Still, I stayed with my strategy. Every time he stopped one of my nukes, I launched three more. Trujillo's planes were just circling around with nothing to do. He had to use all his concentration to defend Cantania.

Finally, I managed to get one nuke past him,

and half of Cantania turned gray. One more good shot and the game would be mine.

After five minutes, I had only ten nukes left — three in my submarines, three in my bombers, and four in my ground-based launchers. I could have fired them one at a time, rotating them to try and confuse Trujillo. But he was so fast with his shield. I decided to just let them all fly in one all-out, last-ditch attack.

I pushed the button and breathed a sigh of relief as the missiles left their bases. From my point of view, my game was over. If one of my nukes hit the target, I would win the game. If Trujillo stopped them all, he would win. It was out of my hands. I hit the trigger one last time just to make sure I was out of ammo. Nothing happened. My missiles were all gone.

I'm not sure if Trujillo noticed that I had stopped firing. He was concentrating heavily on the screen. Those last ten nukes were streaking toward Cantania, plus ten or twenty I had fired earlier.

Trujillo flicked his shield around the screen, blocking my nukes milliseconds before they would have reached their targets. He was like the goalie on a bad hockey team, stopping shot after shot on goal. He couldn't keep it up forever, I figured. At some point, one of my shots would have to make it through.

With just a few remaining nukes on the screen, one of them did get through. It was a sub-based missile I had launched from pretty far out in the Atlantic. Trujillo ignored it so he could stop my other missiles, and by the time he got his shield back to stop this one, it was too late.

"Go, baby!" I shouted.

The missile missed his shield by a pixel or two and crashed into Cantania. A big mushroom cloud rose over the country.

GAME OVER, the screen read, as the American national anthem played. CANTANIA HAS BEEN DESTROYED. THE UNITED STATES RULES THE WORLD.

I relaxed in my chair, exhausted from concentrating so hard. I looked over at Trujillo for the first time since the game began. He was sweating and breathing heavily. He threw down his controller in disgust.

"Good game," I said.

I pressed the intercom button and notified the captain that Supreme Ruler Trujillo and I had completed our negotiations. Almost immediately, the door opened.

"Captain," I said calmly as I picked up my briefcase, "Mr. Trujillo and I have resolved our differences. Please notify our respective governments. There is no need for us to go to war. No need for soldiers to die. The crisis is over. Cantania's forces will retreat."

"Never!" Trujillo shouted. Suddenly, he came up behind me and grabbed me around the neck so his forearm was wrapped tightly around my windpipe.

"Give me the football!" he shouted in my ear.

"What football?" I choked. "I don't have a football."

"The briefcase with your nuclear codes!" he yelled. "Give it to me or I will kill you."

I let go of the briefcase and he took it with his other hand.

"That's a good boy," Trujillo said, keeping a firm grip on my throat.

"Mr. President!" the captain exclaimed.

"Make one move and the President is dead!" Trujillo shouted at the captain. "I control the President of the United States and its nuclear arsenal. How does it feel, President Moon? Without your planes and guns and bombs, the United States is powerless."

"The minute you walk out of this room you'll be killed," I choked out.

"I'm not afraid to die!" Trujillo gloated. "Can you say the same, President Moon? Because you're going to be my human shield until we get back to Cantania. There I will parade you through the streets for the entertainment of my people."

"We had a deal," I choked.

"Did you really think I was going to give up because you beat me in a *video game*?" Trujillo laughed. "Foolish boy."

How stupid I was! How could I allow myself to be alone in a room with a ruthless dictator and no Secret Service agents to protect me in case he tried anything?

At that moment the image of Agent John Doe flashed through my mind. He was still in the hospital after the attempt on my life. If only Doe were here, he would kick Trujillo's butt.

Wait!

Doe had taught me the Secret Ninja Death Touch! It was the deadliest system of self-defense ever created! He told me it was only to be used in life-or-death situations. If this wasn't a life-or-death situation, nothing was.

I reached behind and pressed my thumb on that certain part of Trujillo's body, the neurological shutdown point where you can disrupt an attacker's nervous and circulatory systems.

"Hey!" Trujillo shouted. "Get your hand off me!"

"You get *your* hand off *me*," I replied, as I pressed harder. The pressure of his arm around my neck loosened a bit as Trujillo struggled to push my hand away.

I pressed harder. Trujillo gasped and a few seconds later fell backward. He slumped to the floor, slamming his head on the table on the way down. By the time he hit the ground, he was unconscious.

Front page of The Washington Post, *December 30:*

MOON BEATS TRUJILLO AT HIS OWN GAME: CANTANIAN LEADER HUMILIATED, FORCES RETREAT, WAR AVERTED

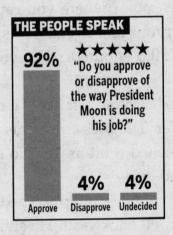

THE PEOPLE SPEAK

92%

★★★★★
"Do you approve or disapprove of the way President Moon is doing his job?"

Approve

4%
Disapprove

4%
Undecided

27.
★ A Hero ★

After I beat Trujillo at the World War Four game, he was so humiliated that the citizens of Cantania overthrew him and installed a new government elected by the people.

And me, well, when I arrived back in Washington on New Year's Day, everybody treated me like I was Armstrong just back from the moon. (*Neil* Armstrong, that is.) People lined the streets for miles, cheering and clapping their hands. Hundreds of thousands of letters poured into the White House. Everybody loved me again.

MOON IS HERO! the headlines shouted. Video game sales zoomed. Hollywood wanted to turn my life into a movie.

"You must be butter, 'cause you're on a roll!"

Vice-President Syers said when she hugged me at Andrews Air Force Base.

"It was nothing," I said modestly.

"You did good, Moon. Real good."

"That's all I wanted to do," I replied.

Even my dad, for once in his life, had something nice to say. "Well done," he said as he clapped me on the back. Of course, Dad also says that when he orders meat in a restaurant, but I took it as a compliment.

The most surprising reaction I got was from the First Lady. Chelsea had always treated me like I was a dork. But when I got back from my confrontation with Trujillo, she ran over, threw her arms around me, and kissed me right on the lips.

"You were so brave!" she gushed. Even after I was able to pry her off me, she kept looking at me with goo-goo eyes.

Jeez! I didn't see what all the fuss was about. All I did was win a dumb video game.

The first year of my presidency was just about over. There was only one thing left to do.

Traditionally, every January the President of

the United States stands before Congress to give what is called the State of the Union Address. It's a speech in which the President talks about how things are going in the country. He discusses problems facing the nation and says what he thinks should be done to solve them. The speech is televised and just about everybody watches it.

I called up Lane and begged him to come back and write the State of the Union Address for me, but he wouldn't do it. He said I was doing a great job on my own, and I should keep doing it that way.

I had never written a speech before. But I sat down and wrote this one myself. I spent a lot of time on it and wouldn't let anyone else see it. Not my parents. Not Chelsea. Not even Vice-President Syers.

So there I was on January 9, standing alone behind the big podium inside the Capitol Building. In front of me, in a huge semicircle, sat a sea of elected officials. All one hundred members of the Senate. Four hundred and thirty-five members of the House of Representatives.

Sitting behind me were Vice-President Syers and the Speaker of the House. Up in the balcony were my parents and Chelsea with her folks. Secret Service Agent Doe was there, just out of the hospital and recovering nicely. White House Chief Usher Honeywell was there. I had even invited Miller the Killer.

At exactly eight o'clock the red light on the TV camera went on and a hush fell over the huge room.

"Well," I began, "it has been an exciting year!"

The crowd laughed good-naturedly and then broke into applause.

"My fellow Americans, all I wanted when I accepted the presidency was to do good for America. Some things have worked out. Other things haven't. I want you to know that I tried my best."

Again, the crowd broke into hearty applause.

"I learned a lot this year. I learned a lot about what it means to be President of the United States. Being President isn't about riding around in limousines and helicopters to get your picture taken. It's about doing the right thing for the people.

"This, I learned, isn't as easy as I thought it

would be. I learned that no matter what you do, a lot of people are going to be angry. Let me give you some examples. The President has to find a way to protect the nation's forests and also protect the job of a man who makes his living cutting down trees. The President has to help the poor without penalizing people who worked hard to become rich. The President has to work to end prejudice and also protect a bigot's freedom of speech. The President has to reduce people's taxes without taking away the services people need.

"These problems are so difficult and complicated, it may be impossible to solve them. I know one thing — I can't solve 'em.

"So, in the spirit of doing what is good for America, I would like to do one more good thing for my country as my first year as President comes to a close."

I paused and took a deep breath.

"Effective tomorrow morning," I said slowly, "I resign as President of the United States."

The crowd broke into loud guffawing.

"That *wasn't* a joke," I insisted. "I *mean* it. I quit."

There was a loud gasp, then silence in the great hall. Not a sound. And then, two loud thuds were heard. It was my mom fainting and hitting the ground, followed almost immediately by Chelsea.

"I learned a lot this past year," I continued as medics rushed to revive Mom and Chelsea. "And the most important thing I learned was that I'm not ready for the responsibility of the presidency. That's why I've decided to resign."

"You can't!" somebody shouted.

"But I did," I said. "I'd like Vice-President Syers to join me on the podium at this time. Mr. Honeywell, will you please help Mrs. Syers?"

Honeywell hurried behind me to push Vice-President Syers' wheelchair down to the podium. He was about to return to his seat, but I asked him to stay.

"Vice-President Syers," I said as I pulled out a Bible. "Will you raise your right hand, please, and repeat after me? I, June Syers . . ."

"I, June Syers . . ."

"Do solemnly swear . . ."

"Do solemnly swear . . ."

"That I will faithfully execute the Office of President of the United States . . ."

"That I will faithfully execute the Office of President of the United States . . ."

"And will, to the best of my ability . . ."

"And will, to the best of my ability . . ."

"Preserve, protect, and defend . . ."

"Preserve, protect, and defend . . ."

"The Constitution of the United States."

"The Constitution of the United States."

The crowd erupted into tremendous applause as Mrs. Syers smiled and waved.

There was one last thing I wanted to do before stepping off the stage. I moved Honeywell next to President Syers.

"My fellow Americans," I said into the microphone, "I don't know if I brought our nation together in the last year, but I *do* know this: These two fine people were brought together. And we are gathered here not just to swear in a new President, but also to join this man and this woman in holy matrimony. If anyone here sees a reason why this man and woman should not be wed, let them speak now or forever hold their peace."

"You go, girl!" somebody hooted from the balcony.

I continued, "Do you, President Syers, promise to love, honor, and cherish this man, Roger Honeywell, as your lawfully wedded husband until death do you part?"

"I do," Mrs. Syers said happily.

"And do you, Roger Honeywell, take this fine woman to be your lawfully wedded wife, in sickness and in health, until death do you part?"

"I do," Mr. Honeywell said proudly.

"By the power vested in me as President of the United States, I now pronounce you husband and wife. Mr. Honeywell, you may kiss the President, I mean, the bride."

When Mrs. Syers was finished smooching with Honeywell, she carefully struggled out of her wheelchair and rose to her feet, leaning on the podium for support.

"Well, I guess I seen just about everything now," she said. The crowd cheered for a full five minutes.

"When I was a little girl," Mrs. Syers went on, "if anybody ever said that an old, black, handi-capped lady would someday be President of the

United States, they would have been locked up in the loony bin. Don't this beat all?"

The crowd erupted into applause once again.

"Over sixty years ago, Franklin Delano Roosevelt was standing here delivering his last State of the Union Address. Most of you weren't around then or were too young to remember. But I remember. Roosevelt was my hero. He couldn't stand up too good, either. He had polio, you see, and he was a sick old man by then. But he was a force, that man! He didn't take no sass from *nobody*. He made people believe they could accomplish *anything*. Didn't matter if they were rich or poor. Didn't matter if they were black or white, young or old, man or woman, pretty or ugly, educated or not.

"Well, I'm living proof that in the United States of America, anybody can go anywhere. Be anything. So you better be ready, America. 'Cause Roosevelt is back. And I'm him. Thank you."

And that was that.

When I stepped off the podium, the reporters were all over me like a swarm of gnats. They wanted to know why I decided to resign when I had the highest approval rating of any President in American history. I just shrugged my shoulders. Sometimes a guy's gotta do what he's gotta do.

The next day, Mom, Dad, and I packed up our stuff and moved back to Wisconsin. I would be going back to my old school, back to my old friends, back to my old life as a regular kid.

But, like I said, it had been an exciting year!

★ Nice Try! ★

Hi, there, pea brain! You thought you were pretty smart, didn't you — turning to the back of the book to see how the story turned out.

Did you really think I was going to give away the ending so easily? Ha! You should be ashamed of yourself. Now turn back to page five and start reading.

Anything worth doing is worth doing right.

Learn how it all began for
President Judson Moon in

THE KID WHO
★ RAN FOR ★
PRESIDENT

It was a bright, sunny Saturday morning. Lane showed up at nine o'clock, wheeling June Syers, who was holding an enormous basket of lemons on her lap.

My folks were already gone for the day, attending seminars to help them sell more carpet tiles and cardboard boxes.

"I hate suits," I said, pulling at my collar.

"You look outstanding," Lane said. "Very presidential."

Lane and I set up a long table at the edge of the lawn and Mrs. Syers got to work making lemonade.

I dug some long sticks of wood out of the basement and nailed cardboard to them. Lane has nicer handwriting than I do, so he painted three signs: MOON & JUNE FOR PRESIDENT, HELP US! WE NEED $20 MILLION! and LEMONADE 25 CENTS.

"Twenty million dollars?" whistled Mrs. Syers. "I'm gonna need more lemons."

"It's just a symbol," Lane explained, blowing up balloons to hang on the booth. "Grown-ups get all misty-eyed when they see lemonade stands. It reminds 'em of the good old days."

"There *were* no good old days," harumphed Mrs. Syers. "The good old days is anything that happens before you're old enough to see the world as it really is."

I live on a pretty busy street. Cars started pulling over right away and soon our lemonade stand was surrounded by people.

"Hi!" I said to each person cheerfully. "My name is Judson Moon. I'm twelve years old and I'm running for President of the YOU-nited States."

"Keep smiling," Lane whispered in my ear. "And don't say anything that will make anybody angry. Kiss some babies."

"I'm not really into kissing," I complained. "Do I have to?"

"Then hug people."

"I'm not very good at it," I admitted. "I never know which side I should put my head. If I put my head toward the left and if the other person puts her head toward the right, we bump heads. Can't I just punch 'em on the arm?"

We never had the chance to solve the problem. A beat-up Chevy Nova pulled up, followed by a minivan. A sloppily dressed guy got out of the Nova. He was carrying a pad in his hand and a pencil behind his ear.

"Judson Moon?" he said, sticking out his hand. "My name is Pete Guerra, with the *Cap Times*. I figured you wouldn't mind if I brought a few of the TV newsboys with me."

A couple of guys got out of the minivan lugging video cameras, still cameras, a tripod, tape recorder, and microphone. They took a bunch of pictures of me serving people lemonade, and then Lane ushered us off to the side so Pete Guerra could interview me.

"So why ya running for President, kid?"

"Well, I figure grown-ups have had the last one thousand years to mess up the world. Now it's our turn."

"That's a good quote," Guerra said, looking

up from the pad he was scribbling on. "Did you think of that yourself or did your campaign manager feed it to you?"

"Lane's job is to run the campaign," I explained. "My job, as a candidate for the highest office in our nation, is to come up with good quotes."

"Ya got any pets, kid?"

"A parakeet," I replied. "Her name is Sn — Cuddles," I lied.

"Okay, let's get down to more serious business, Judson. People are going to want to know what positions you take."

"I play third base," I said. "Sometimes I'll play the outfield if the coach needs me out there."

Guerra rolled his eyes and shook his head from side to side. "No, I mean your positions on the *issues*. Your *opinions*. Like, what do you think about gun control?"

"Guns don't kill people. They usually just cause serious injuries."

"What about race?"

"I love all the races. My dream is to see the Indianapolis 500 and the Kentucky Derby someday."

"What's the first thing you plan to do when you become President?"

"Install a skateboard ramp in the Oval Office and redecorate the White House with heavy metal posters."

"When did you decide to run for President, Judson?"

"When I found out the White House had a bowling alley."

When Guerra had enough of my wisecracks, he moved over to June Syers, who was dispensing her worldview for free with every cup of lemonade.

"Mrs. Syers," asked Guerra. "How did you become Judson Moon's running mate?"

"Musta been my good looks and sparkling personality," she said.

"Does Moon have what it takes to lead the country?"

"He can't hardly do any worse than the fools who are runnin' it now, can he?" she said. Then she proceeded to give him a capsule history of the United States, which basically consisted of saying the Indians were fools, the Pilgrims were fools, the Founding Fathers were fools, the Union and the Confederacy were fools, and every politician except Franklin D. Roosevelt was a fool.

"And I oughta know," she concluded, "'cause I lived through all of 'em."

As soon as Guerra and the TV guys left, Lane began tearing down our stand. Mrs. Syers counted up the money, and proudly announced that we had raised sixty-five dollars. There was a lot more lemonade we could have sold, but Lane wasn't interested.

"The idea wasn't to sell lemonade," he said. "The idea was to make news. The money will come later."

"Turn on channel three!" Lane shouted breathlessly into the phone that night while I was eating dinner.

Dad and Mom didn't seem to be paying attention to the TV, so I switched channels.

"After these messages," the anchorman bellowed, "we'll tell you about a twelve-year-old boy who says he's running for President. Stay tuned."

"Where do they get these stupid stories?" Dad muttered from behind his newspaper.

I didn't say a word. I wanted to see the look on his face. After three commercials, the news anchor came back on.

"Well, they say that in America any youngster can grow up to be President. But at least one youngster isn't going to wait. Twelve-year-old Judson Moon of Madison is throwing his baseball cap into the ring right *now*."

Mom and Dad actually lowered their newspapers and looked at the TV. My face filled the screen and Dad's jaw fell open. Mom dropped the glass she was holding and it shattered on the floor.

"Grown-ups have had the last one thousand years to mess up the world," I heard myself say. "Now it's our turn."

"Moon will be running as a third party candidate representing 'The Lemonade Party,' for the Presidency in November," the anchor-man continued. "The sixth-grader and his running mate — an elderly African-American woman named June Syers — have already collected the two thousand signatures they need to get on the ballot in Wisconsin, and they're raising money by selling lemonade at a stand in front of Judson's house. We asked Mr. Moon how he plans to get around the Constitution, which clearly states that a candidate must be thirty-five years of age to run for the Presidency."

"I'm actually thirty-six," I said to the camera with a smirk. "I'm just extremely young for my age."

"That's our news for tonight. Good night and may all *your* news be good news."

Before Mom or Dad could say a word, the phone rang. It was my Aunt Lucy.

"Am I hallucinating!?" she shrieked. "Or did I just see you on TV?"

The instant I hung up the phone with Aunt Lucy, it rang again. It was one of my teachers. When I hung up with her, the phone rang again. Kids from school were calling. Mom's friends were calling. Total strangers were calling. Finally, Dad took the phone off the hook.

"Is this one of your pranks?" he asked. I wasn't sure if he was angry or amused.

"It's *sort* of a prank," I replied. "I don't expect to win or anything. You're always telling me I should get involved with extracurricular activities. Well . . ."

"I meant you should join the chess club or the school paper or something!" he said, his voice rising. "I didn't mean you should run for President!"

"Why didn't you tell us, dear?" asked Mom.

"I *did* tell you, Mom. You just weren't listening."

"Well, I think it's cute, honey," she said, "as long as it doesn't interfere with your schoolwork. Remember, homework first, running for President second."

Dad just rolled his eyes and shook his head slowly from side to side.

In the morning, I got up early and rushed outside to get the paper. There I was on the front page, with this big smile on my face, pouring some lady a cup of lemonade. There was an article to go with the photo:

MOON MISSION: 12-year-old on Quest for White House
By Peter Guerra

While other boys his age are flipping baseball cards and dyeing their hair purple, Judson Moon has other things on his mind — like running for President of the United States.

The 12-year-old from Madison says he is disillusioned with the Republicans and Democrats and has decided to mount a campaign as a third party candidate in November's election.

"Grown-ups have had a thousand years to mess up the world," claims Moon. "Now it's our turn."

The young man, outfitted in a suit and tie, was raising money on Saturday by selling lemonade in front of his house for 25 cents a cup. He will have to sell 180 million cups to raise $20 million, the figure he says he needs to mount a national campaign.

Moon's running mate and fellow lemonade saleswoman is Mrs. June Syers, a retired nurse who used to baby-sit for the candidate.

"We're a perfect team," Moon says. "I'm young and she's old. I'm white and she's black. I'm dumb and she's smart."

Watch out, Democrats! Stand back, Republicans! Here comes The Lemonade Party!

Word gets around fast. When I walked into school on Monday morning, it was like I was from another planet. Everywhere I went, everybody was looking at me, pointing, and whispering. I'd walk toward a crowd of kids and they'd part to let me through.

Pretty weird!

Abby wished me good luck. Several of the teachers gave me the thumbs-up sign. Even Chelsea came over to me.

"You weren't kidding about running for President, were you?" she said, a lot friendlier than she was when we met.

"No, I wasn't," I replied. "You weren't kidding about being First Lady, were you?"

"Actually I *was*," she said. "But now that I know you're really doing this, you can count on me."

Arthur Krantz made a face when he saw me, and I made the same face right back at him. As every politician knows, you can't please everybody.

★ About the Author ★

Dan Gutman is the author of many books for young readers, such as *The Kid Who Ran for President*, *Honus and Me*, *The Million Dollar Shot*, and *They Came from Centerfield*. He lives in Haddonfield, New Jersey, with his wife, Nina, and their children, Sam and Emma.

If you'd like to find out more about Dan, his books, or his school visits, visit his Web site (www.dangutman.com).